Praise fo

MW00880376

"Lots of thrills and chills grace the pages. When they aren't fighting or running from evil they are fighting chemistry--hot, boiling, explosive chemistry. Make the pages even more explosive--the shocking mouth dropping revelations. Clear a block of time, get comfy and enjoy. You will not want to stop. There will be no coming back later because you will want to know everything. And everything is worth it."

—*Trudy, Amazon*

"Draven was a great fast read …You were waiting to turn the next page to see what happened next. Once again Patricia has you hook line and sinker. The books keep getting better and better."

—*Joey, GoodReads*

"Unique, action packed, and a match made in Heaven."

—*Karen, SiK Reviews*

"Lots of hot and sexy, but lots of WTF and OMG at the same time. Great novella to keep us reading and wanting more until Xander gets here."

—*dustdevil93 Amazon*

"I have to say this again if you love J.R. Ward's Black Dagger Brotherhood series then you will want together devour the Sons of Sangue series!"

—*Christy, Amazon*

Draven

Sons of Sangue

Patricia A. Rasey

Dedication

To Jackie Ferrell and Stacy Affleck, I thank you for helping me find those last minute pesky typos.

To my editor, Catherine Snodgrass, who puts up with my it will be there tomorrow. *Thanks for moving things around for me and all your hard work.*

Thank you to my family who puts up with my hectic schedules.

Acknowledgements

Thank you to my cover artist, Frauke Spanuth, from Croco Designs for creating the Sons of Sangue covers, and making each cover "my favorite to date."

CHAPTER ONE

A BULLET WHIZZED PAST HIS EAR, STINGING THE FLESH.
"Fuck!" Draven Smith ran faster, dodging a few low-hanging branches and pulling Brea Gotti along behind him. Wetness welled to the surface of his ear and ran down the shell, telling him he'd been grazed. "Just who the hell's Wheaties did you piss in?"

"I hate to be the bearer of bad news, but I don't think it's me they're aiming at." While his breath sawed out of him, her breath was even, undisturbed by their scurry through the dense forest. "You want me to carry you?"

A humorless laugh barked out of him. "Great. Why not take my man-card while you're at it?"

He felt her humor. He didn't have to look back to see it. Damn maddening woman. "How about we get the fuck out of here while I'm still alive?"

"I won't let you die."

He rolled his eyes, though she'd never see it since he still led the way.

Death or vampire.

Well, if that wasn't a pisser.

Draven grumbled, "Let's try keeping me alive."

Another bullet whipped through the leaves above him, raining vegetation down around them.

1

Fuck!

A few days ago he'd been serving drinks at his club, The Blood 'n' Rave, and he had been damn happy to do so. Now it felt like a lifetime ago as he ran for his life. Of course not Brea's, since only a bullet striking her directly through the heart, and stopping her vampire blood from flowing, would take her down. Nope, he was definitely running for his life.

What the hell had he been thinking when he had packed up a few necessities, no more than a week ago at most, and dragged her from the backroom of his club? Draven chuckled with a shake of his head. Hell, he had not one thing to offer in the way of help. She'd likely wind up having to save his sorry human ass.

Her godfather, Raúl Trevino Caballero, Mexican kingpin of the La Paz Cartel, apparently wanted Brea pretty damn bad to send his goons after her. Draven didn't have a clue as to Raúl's intension. And if Brea was being honest with him, neither did she.

Not to mention the Sons of Sangue MC had been in the dark about Brea's existence. Should they find out about her, and the fact he'd kept that knowledge from them, they'd no doubt want a piece of his ass as well.

Brea Gotti was the daughter of a mob boss, with connections to the Sons' sworn enemy. The MC had wanted Raúl's head and rightly so. The kingpin played a huge role in the death of Kane "Viper" Tepes's only son. Kane and Kaleb "Hawk" Tepes, his twin and the president of the MC, had been gunning for the man ever since. And all because Kane's ex-ol' lady was a bitch and had gotten into bed with the wrong damn people.

Vampire or not, the Caballero brothers had managed to kill Ion and left Rosalee to suffer. The Sons had taken Raúl's brother as penance, but it hadn't been enough. Kane and Kaleb wouldn't rest until the planet was wiped free of the filth and greed the man spread. Greed Draven had at one-time profited from, until the Sons forbade him to sell drugs from his establishment any longer.

Christ! That seemed like eons ago.

Mix in the DEA, with their offered deal to save Draven from prosecution if he went undercover to take down the Sons' rival MC, the Devils, and he had landed in one hell of a pile of shit.

Draven shook his head.

The whole thing had become a complete cluster fuck to be sure, and the Devils probably wanted their share of him too.

Well, get in the fucking line.

Another bullet whizzed past, this one grazing his shoulder and bringing his thoughts back to the present. "Son of a bitch."

Blood leaked from the flesh wound. Not a gusher, but enough that he feared Brea's vampire genetics making a sudden appearance. At the moment, they had no idea who chased them. He'd bet whoever they were, they had no clue what Brea could become when she got good and pissed.

This close to Mexico, Draven was pretty sure it was Raúl's goons shooting at him. He still hadn't figured out who had killed her mate, Joseph "Kinky" Sala, or why the murdering bastard felt the need to end the biker's life. The hitman had shot Brea's mate in the head, a bullet that stopped the vampire's heart from beating, and had killed him on the spot outside of Draven's night club.

Whoever fired at them now, correction … *him*, Draven bet they were one in the same.

Dodging beneath a low hanging branch and taking a quick left, Brea and Draven headed farther into the dense foliage. If they could put enough distance between him and whoever the hell was chasing them, he might be able to find them a place to hide and thus lose the tail.

Ditching his beloved Chevy Camaro at a rest stop miles back near the border no longer seemed like a wise idea. He hadn't disagreed that his car would be recognizable, but damn if he hadn't argued like a two-year-old at the idea of leaving it behind. Once they had taken to foot, someone had begun quickly trailing them and the gunfire had begun. Obviously, the Camaro had been spotted long before they'd ditched it.

Brea tugged on Draven's hand so hard he damn near flew backward. Her chest bumped into his back. She had gotten his attention all right. When he looked back, he saw her in full, scary-as-fuck vampire mode.

"What the hell?"

"It's the scent of your blood." She shrugged with a grave grin. "It's been four days."

Her skin had taken on the death chill—the translucent appearance of a vampire's flesh when too much time had passed between feedings. Draven groaned, knowing full well it would be his blood she next feasted on. The bright side to letting her dip her fangs would be the rock-hard erection she would give him. The downside would be the huge case of blue balls he'd be plagued with. By now he should be getting used to it. All he had to do was look at her and his dick was at half-mast. Acting on his desire wasn't going to be an option, though, not when she had been Joseph's mate, not when she hadn't been given proper time to mourn.

No matter what his libido had to say about the matter.

Without warning, Brea wrapped her arms around his waist, knocking the breath from him. She bent at the knees, leaping higher than humanly possible, and landed with a thud on a thick branch of a very tall oak, turning Draven's ankle. She placed her hand over his mouth to keep him from screaming like a girl. Grabbing onto a branch above her head to steady herself, she pressed a finger to her lips, indicating he should be quiet. Draven would've much rather she silenced him with her bow-shaped lips. Teetering because of his wayward thoughts, he quickly wrapped his arms around the center of the oak and prayed they would go unnoticed this high up into the branches.

A few silent moments later four men passed beneath, all carrying assault rifles and wearing camouflage clothing. They scanned the forest, the barrels of the rifles doing a sweep of the area. Draven held his breath, afraid to breathe for fear of disturbing the leaves and blowing their cover. Finally, about the time he thought he might pass out from the lack of oxygen and topple atop the goons, the men continued on their way.

Positive they were now out of earshot, he shifted position, trying to alleviate his weight off his sore ankle, and let out a moan. He lowered himself to the large branch, straddling it and taking his weight off the injured foot. His blood roared through his veins and pulsed in his ears.

Fuck! That had been close.

"You okay?" Brea asked, barely above a whisper.

"I've been better. Thanks." Draven couldn't keep the smart ass from entering his tone if he tried.

His entire fucking life had been turned upside down, not to mention barely escaping with it just a few short minutes ago, and all because Joseph had thought to entrust him with his mate's care if something should happen to him. Not that he hadn't enjoyed her company, or that she hadn't been a huge fucking turn on. It was the part that had his knees knocking as tremors of fear ran down his spine he wasn't much too fond of.

And all because Brea Gotti had entered his life.

At this point, he was thinking his chances were far better with the Devils and the DEA. Shit! These cartel goons were fucking dangerous. Messing with them was like stirring up a hive of angry hornets.

"Look, I'm sorry I brought you into this mess." Brea lowered herself so that she mounted the branch in front of him. "I'm sure your car is still sitting back at the rest stop. Why not track back? I can do this on my own, Draven. I really don't need you. The last thing I want on my conscience is your death. I already have Kinky's."

"You aren't doing this alone, Brea. For whatever reason, Kinky thought you should contact me if something happened to him. I'm not about to let him down."

Brea took in a deep breath and looked through the trees. "If I have to drag you along, that means I not only have to watch out for myself but you as well."

"Ouch. That hurts." He rubbed his sternum. Draven wasn't a body builder by any means, but he wasn't a pushover either. He had bounced a few people in his day. But the cartel? That was some serious shit! "You watch out for yourself, Brea. I don't need a woman coming to my rescue."

"Not even if that woman is a vampire and at least ten times stronger than you?" She winked at him, offering him a slight tip of her lips. "Let's get the hell out of this tree and get on our way then."

"You still bent on visiting your godfather?"

"I am. Nothing you say will stop me."

"So why the hell are we running from his lackeys?"

"Because you dope, they may not harm me, but they'd have no problem taking you out." She pulled her lower lip between her teeth. "Besides, I want the element of surprise on my side. I want to see my godfather on my terms, not with a dozen of his men surrounding him. I want to look in his eyes when he tells me he didn't order the hit on Kinky."

Without waiting for a response, she slid from the branch and jumped to the forest floor as if they were only ten feet in the air. Draven looked down from his perch. If he jumped, he'd no certain break a leg.

"Well? What are you waiting for?"

"You wouldn't happen to have a ladder handy?"

Brea chuckled. "Nope."

"Rope?"

"Nope."

"Then how to you expect me to get down?"

"Jump."

"You can't be serious."

Even from his height, he saw the twinkle in her gaze. "Don't worry. I'll catch you."

Draven shook his head. Yep, by the time this little adventure came to an end, he might as well hand over his balls. Leaning to the side, he dangled his feet over the branch, hanging by his fingertips.

"You waiting on Christmas?" Her feminine tone mocked him.

"You really know how to unman a guy, don't you?"

Hearing her answering chuckle, he let go of the branch.

CHAPTER TWO

"WHAT IS THIS PLACE?" DRAVEN ASKED, FOLLOWING her through the old wooden door.

Brea used the key still hidden under the rock beside the steps. The overgrown vegetation made it obvious no one had been here in quite some time. Her family used to come here when she was a child anytime her father needed to lie low from the states.

"Back when the trial was going on for Great Uncle John, my dad brought us all here for the first time. We stayed for a year before returning. My dad later took over the family business."

Draven scratched his nape. "That was quite a while ago. You couldn't have been very old."

"I was only a year old when the feds locked up my great uncle. My grandfather was ten years his senior and my father was in his early twenties when he had me. He was pretty young for a crime boss."

"How did you ever remember this place?"

"We came back often. Anytime my father had business with my godfather, we stayed here."

She looked around, memories assailing her. It was as if she could still reach out and touch them. Nothing had changed. The same floral sofa sat against the roughhewn

9

walls. The old, round wooden table they all sat around to eat meals sat to the left of it. Brea walked over, traced her fingers over the words carved into the surface and smiled. Her father had wanted to discipline her, but the "I 'heart shape' my daddy," she had carved into the wood when she was ten made it hard for him to scold her. She smiled at the memory.

Her father had a large, booming voice that commanded respect, but whenever he spoke to her, he used to lower his tone. *"Brea, you can't be marking up momma's things. But I love you too, with whatever love I have to give."* He had placed a kiss on her forehead with the spoken words.

Brea looked back at Draven, the memories fading from her vision. "My father passed away when I was in my late teens. With Great Uncle John's and my grandfather's death several years earlier, the family business was passed on to a man related to the crime boss Gotti had killed when he took over the family. In the meantime, the cartel's presence in the states grew. They no longer did business with the Gambinos after my father died.

"My mom had died when I was eleven. They told me it was a car accident. I always suspected it was something far more sinister. My father had become damn near unreachable after that. When he passed away, I tried to stay away from it all. I began to distance myself from my godfather, even though he was all I had left of my family. That's when I met Kinky."

Draven reached up and pulled the tie from his hair. His thick waves fell about his shoulders. He picked out a few leaves and used his fingers to try and straighten it the best he could. With his long waves, brown eyes, and trim build, he was exactly Brea's type. As a matter of fact, she found the bar owner to be damn hot. From the moment she'd walked into his club looking for Joseph, she found herself attracted to the man. Too bad they hadn't met under better circumstances. He had that dark, sort of Goth style about him. Brea could easily see him dressing in platform shoes and rimming his eyes with kohl.

Joseph had been quite the opposite, but she'd loved him nonetheless. He had taken her in when she had nowhere else to go. He had respected her age and treated her like a princess. He had come to mean everything to her. He had been a father figure first, protecting her from the bad world she had been a part of, to the caring lover she later found in him. It had taken a couple of years of begging to finally get her way. But in the end, she had become his mate.

Brea never once regretted her decision, even if there were times she thought he might. No one could make her laugh or feel more loved than Joseph. She had quickly become his everything and he would have stopped at nothing to protect her. Even though things had begun to shift in their relationship, his death was a huge blow to her heart, leaving a hole she doubted could ever be filled again. Nor did she want to. Joseph deserved to be remembered for the good times.

"He took you in."

"When I had nothing and no one." A lone tear slipped down her cheek. She smiled weakly. "Now I'm back to where

I started. I don't understand my godfather's sudden obsession and need to chase after me. I haven't heard from him in years. It's not like I kept in touch with him. I hate him for Kinky. He had nothing to do with my relationship with my godfather. I know it's not yet proven, but my heart tells me Raúl is at fault."

"When he called you, you said Raúl asked if you had learned your lesson. What was that about?"

She shook her head, moistening her lips with her tongue. "I can only assume he blamed Kinky for keeping me from him. What other reason could he possibly have for killing a man who meant nothing to him."

"And now he blames me."

Brea knew it wasn't a question. She had said as much to Draven the night they had fled his nightclub. She should've never gotten him involved. Raúl Trevino Caballero was a very bad man, worse than any of the men involved in her family's business. Last she heard, he was responsible for over twenty thousand deaths in Mexico and beyond. He was not a man you wanted to piss off. Maybe it was time to cut her losses, send Draven back to Oregon, and go it alone to her godfather's. No one was safe with her, and especially not someone with human DNA.

If Draven wouldn't leave on his own, she would devise a plan and head out without him. They could lie low here for a few days while she figured out exactly what she was going to do. Draven might not like it, but she would not be responsible for another death. Raúl's vacation home wasn't far from here.

She could easily make the distance on foot. Draven would only slow her down. Once she left, he could find his way back to the border and his car.

Her heart weighed heavy. Leaving him wasn't something she wanted to do, but she had little choice. She couldn't worry about protecting him, when she needed to keep herself alive while she got close to her godfather, close enough to take his life with her bare hands, or her fangs. Brea didn't care which, as long as the end result was the same. Raúl Trevino Caballero would not live to kill another human being. He needed to be stopped, and she was just the person to do it.

"We'll lie low here for a few days."

"Raúl doesn't know about this place?"

She shook her head. "My father never fully trusted the man, and rightfully so. With Raúl it was always best to keep a few secrets. Daddy would never have put his family at risk to get what he wanted."

Draven patted the sofa, sending a dust cloud into the space separating them. "This place could use a good cleaning."

She thought of his pristine white apartment, knowing he'd feel more than a little uncomfortable in the years of dirt layering the place. "We can clean it. It's not as bad as it looks. Just a little surface dust."

"And food?" One of his dark brows rose. Damn if even the slight arch of his brow wasn't turning her on at the moment. She needed to feed. "Yours might be taken care of, but what am I supposed to do for nourishment? My stomach is growling like a malnourished lion at the moment."

"There's a store about ten miles west of here."

He groaned. "I don't think I'm ready for another trek through the woods at the moment, not with my sore ankle. Maybe after we get some sleep. I'll just have to suck it up, and we can go in the morning."

"I'll tell you what. How about I make you a deal?"

"Why do I get the feeling I'm not going to like this?"

Brea smiled, trying not to laugh and make light of his aversion to feeding her. "You feed me first, then we'll clean up this place a little. We'll get some sleep. Come morning, I'll run to the store and get you some food."

She could make it to the store easily in no time, but she'd need to take care of her death chill first or she'd be too weak to make the fast sprint through the forest. Taking Draven would only slow her down.

Draven let out a heavy sigh, grabbed his hair band from his wrist, and made a messy knot at the back of his head, exposing his throat. "I sure in the hell hope this place has running water, because after I feed you, I'm going to need a cold shower. A *very cold* shower."

CHAPTER THREE

D RAVEN RESTED HIS HEAD AGAINST THE CORRUGATED metal shower wall as cold water washed over his heated flesh. He hadn't been lying. Following feeding her, he had an erection bordering on painful. Hell, he was still half-hard. And if he allowed himself to think about the sharp points of her fangs drawing blood from him, there would be no amount of cold water that would be of any help.

A groan escaped him.

What the fuck had he gotten himself into?

There were only a few short hours before the sun set, leaving them in total darkness. This far out, there was no electricity or gas, hence the cold shower. He supposed they could light a few candles, put some firewood into the fire-place, but the last thing they needed was to draw attention to the abandoned cabin. When daylight waned, and the night fell upon them, they'd only have the moonlight in which to see.

Brea would be able to see perfectly fine with her enhanced vision, but Draven would be in for a lot of bruised shins. Not to mention what they would do to pass the time. Another groan escaped him as his cock returned to full mast. There was no way of getting around the five finger shuffle.

Draven had a feeling that over the next few weeks, he was going to become pretty good friends with his right fist.

Wrapping his hand around his erection, he slid his hand from root to tip, barely suppressing another groan as Brea's image in full vampire form swam before him. She was no doubt going to be the death of him, figuratively and literally. His balls tightened. He smoothed his hand over the steely length to the satiny tip.

"Draven?"

Fuck!

He supposed he was also going to become friends with the f-bomb as well. "In the shower still."

"You need to make it quick. Hard telling how much water is in the well and we may need to conserve it." Her voice filtered through the wooden door. If she only knew what the hell he had been up to. "You okay in there?"

"I'm fine, Brea." His tone came out a bit harsher than he intended. He let go of his cock and resigned himself for another night of aching balls. "Christ," he said, barely above a whisper.

"Are you sure you're all right?"

He hadn't thought about her super-sonic vampire hearing. *Just fucking great.* "I'll live ... for now. I'll be out in a sec."

He turned the handles and the cold water ceased. Stepping from the wood planked floor, he grabbed a threadbare towel. Draven opened the door and strode into the living area, no longer caring what Brea thought. His erection tented the towel. Water rivulets ran down the sparse hair on his chest.

Her breath caught when she turned to look at him, her gaze stopping on his erection, barely contained by the towel. She licked her lips and her gaze blackened. Her reaction wasn't helping his condition, not one iota.

"What do you expect, Brea?" Draven was happy to see the death chill gone. "If I'm going to continue to feed you, then you'll need to respect my 'alone time.'" He added quotation marks with his fingers on the last two words.

Her cheeks reddened as she averted her gaze. Brea had beautiful baby blues, a perfectly heart-shaped face, and soft bow-shaped lips. He loved her funky style. One side of her hair was shaved close above her right ear, while the left side grew overlong to just below her chin. A diamond stud sparkled from her left nostril. Five stainless steel rings pierced each of her ears, three in the lower lobes and two higher up in the cartilage, making him anxious to find out if she had more.

"I'm sorry. I didn't know that's what you were doing in there."

"You think I just happen to love cold showers?"

The tiniest of smiles slipped up her lips. He caught the gesture. "Just warn me next time."

"What the fuck am I supposed to say? Excuse me, Brea, while I go yank one off? It's embarrassing enough I'm sporting wood around you three-quarters of the time."

"I'm flattered."

Draven rolled his gaze. "I wasn't looking to compliment you. I think you and I both know what my thoughts are when it comes to you. But I respect the relationship you had with Kinky. And because of that, I will never ask anything from you. I will feed you when I have to, but otherwise you're safe from me. I won't force the issue or my desire to have you. All I ask is for you to please fucking respect my alone time."

She nodded, her face even redder than before. "I am so sorry. If you need to finish your … um, shower…"

He shook his head, hands on his hips. "I no longer feel like it. Sort of takes the edge off, you out here knowing what the hell I am doing in there."

"Then would you mind?"

He blinked. "Mind what?"

"Putting some pants on?"

Draven laughed. "I wouldn't mind at all, but they happen to be drying at the moment. Since it's the only pair I had, I washed out the clothes I was wearing and hung them over the rack in the bathroom to dry. I don't have to tell you that they had to be sweat-soaked and smelly. You'll have to deal with me in the towel for the night."

Draven plopped down onto the floral sofa and propped his feet onto the center storage trunk being used at one time for a coffee table. He crossed his legs at the ankles and leaned back against the scratchy material.

A lone bedroom sat off the living area with what appeared to be a full-size bed. Looks like he'd be taking the couch, un-comfy as it was. He hoped to find a spare sheet in some drawer or closet shelf to take the edge off the itchy fabric. No way in hell could both he and Brea fit in the small bed. Even if they could, he'd still opt for the sofa. The more distance he put between them, the better off they'd both be.

Darkness descended quickly this deep into the woods. Brea had opened a couple of windows, but the breeze had completely stopped, leaving the cabin stuffy. Sweat gathered on his flesh even though he wore little to nothing. Add the close proximity to Brea in the mix…

She crossed the room and headed for the bathroom. Her bare feet padded so softly across the wood flooring Draven couldn't detect the sound. It was as if she floated. Brea looked damn sexy in her dark blue skinny jeans and an over-sized gray sweater that frequently slid off one shoulder. She wore a navy bra beneath, if the thin strap was any indication.

Any other time, he would've jumped on the woman, taken advantage of the situation. *Fuck Joseph!* Did the damn vampire even realize what putting him in charge of his mate would do to him? Draven would get through this scary as fuck hike through the woods, find her godfather, and end the insanity. Once Brea took care of Raúl, then they could go their separate ways and the Sons would never have to know about her existence.

Everyone would be happy.

He could return to his life as he knew it.

However, the thought of leaving Brea behind no longer set well with him, left an odd ache in his chest. Even though he had only been in her company a few short days, he was pretty sure happy wouldn't come close to describing his mood when they parted ways.

Draven heard the water start. He crossed his arms behind his head and stared at the back of the wooden door. His imagination easily called up the image of her standing beneath the old shower head, water sluicing over her naked curves. Her hand no doubt followed those same curves, lathering up her flesh, over her pebbled nipples.

"Fuck! Fuck! Fuck!"

Draven sat forward and scrubbed his palms over his eyes. His erection sprang back to life and all he wanted to do was go outside and get some release for his aching balls. Without a doubt, though, about the time he got started, Brea would be done showering and come looking for him, which certainly didn't help his current situation as he now envisioned her watching him masturbate.

He couldn't help wonder what she might think of his Prince Albert piercing. She had plenty of piercings of her own, and he was betting his might work in his favor should she ever lay her cerulean eyes on it.

The water cut short and he had an erection to get rid of. The towel wasn't doing him any favors.

"Grandma's tits. Big ol' saggy balls." *Think, think … shit that disgusts you.* "A baboon's ass."

The door to the bathroom opened and Brea stepped through, wrapped in an old worn terry cloth robe covering her from chin to ankle. Thank goodness, except he was pretty sure she was naked underneath it.

Damn!

Not helping. He shifted in his seat, grabbed the sofa pillow, placed it over his lap, and groaned.

"Did I hear you say something about a baboon's ass out here?" The amusement in her tone told him she likely heard all of his disgusting comments. "Entertaining yourself in the dark?"

"Now if I were entertaining myself, it wouldn't have been a baboon's ass I had in mind."

Her smile was back, along with the slight reddening of her cheeks. She was just so damn adorable when she was embarrassed. "Mind if I join you on the sofa? It's the only other soft seat in the house and I'm not quite ready to turn in for the night. Where are you going to sleep?"

"Right here. You can have the bed to yourself." He patted the cushion beside him and a small amount of dust rose. "Have a seat."

Brea sat, curling into the corner of the couch and tucking one leg beneath her. "Not sure how long we can go undetected here. By now, I'm sure Raúl's men reported back to him that they lost us."

"But you said he didn't know about this place."

She shook her head. "He didn't. Daddy never wanted him to know. He thought it was safer for us should Raúl ever decide my father lost his usefulness. That doesn't mean they won't be combing the woods looking for us."

A sliver of moonlight came through the window, slightly illuminating her where she sat. Brea's gaze lowered to his chest, staying there a bit more than he was comfortable with. He had a monster-size erection to get rid of and her heated gaze wasn't helping. "Like what you see, sweetheart?"

She laughed. "Isn't that what a woman usually asks a man?"

"I'm not the one doing the ogling at the moment."

"Can I help it if you look sexy as hell sitting there in only that towel? Remember, I have vampire DNA running through my veins. It has a tendency to amp up the emotions."

"Emotions meaning desire."

She lowered her gaze again, this time to her hands clasped in her lap. "I haven't had sex, not since a month or so before Kinky's death."

His pulse hammered in his ears. "And you're telling me this because…?"

Her gaze landed back on his. "Because you aren't the only one suffering here, Draven. I can scent your desire. And quite frankly, I want you too."

CHAPTER FOUR

B REA TIPTOED FROM THE BEDROOM ON HER WAY TO THE small kitchenette, not wanting to wake Draven. A brief glance showed he had slept on his back with a forearm slung over his eyes. His broad shoulders barely fit on the old sofa, making her feel bad for her night of comfort. Maybe she should've offered him the other side of the bed. After all, they were adults and could sleep together without having to actually touch one another or have sex.

"I want you too."

Lord, had she really admitted as much? The night had ended there, with heat filling her cheeks and her heading for the bedroom … alone. Draven hadn't so much as moved a muscle. Not a word after her admission. It appeared her dry spell wasn't about to end, which was just as well since she had yet to get over Joseph's death. Even if things had ended on a sour note for them. Not that she hadn't loved Joseph, but sometimes the gaps were just too far to bridge.

Pulling her lower lip between her teeth, she reached into one of the upper cabinets, looking and praying for some coffee that might have been left behind. Any coffee, stale or not, was better than no coffee at all. Brea moved aside some dusty cups and found an aluminum tin in the back. Taking it down from the cupboard, she grabbed the black plastic knob and lifted the lid. Dark grounds filled half the can.

A little more rooting through cupboards and drawers produced some old circular coffee filters. Brea then opened the cupboard beneath the gas cooktop and prayed to find the propane tank at least partially filled. *Bingo!* Several minutes later and she had coffee percolating on the stove top. The aroma filled the small cabin. Not that she needed substance, thanks to Draven feeding her the night before, but she still loved the smell and taste of a good cup of coffee. The jury was out on whether or not this old percolator would produce the perfect cup or not. Brea leaned more on it being drinkable.

"Is that coffee I smell?"

Brea turned, catching Draven swinging his long, muscular legs to the floor, stretching his arms overhead. A yawn escaped him before he stood and headed in her direction. The white towel still wrapped his lean waist, hanging dangerously low on his hips. Her mouth dried. Damn, if she didn't want some of that. She quickly averted her gaze from his morning wood, her cheeks heating.

Brea rubbed her nape. "Not sure how good it will be."

He chuckled. "How old are those grounds?"

"Quite a few years." She reached up and pulled a couple white mugs from the shelf, rinsed them under the faucet and dried them with a towel she found in the drawer. "I guess we are about to find out how well they held up."

She poured them each a cup, then handed one mug to Draven. He took the coffee to his nose and sniffed.

"Seems passable." He chuckled. Blowing the steam across the surface, he then took a sip. "Not bad."

"I need to run to town and get a few supplies." She took a sip of her own coffee. Not too bad at all. "I think it's best if you stay here."

"I'm not leaving you on your own against those goons out there."

"You're cute." She smiled. "I'm actually better off on my own. I'm glad you feel the need to look out for me, but I can actually move faster if you aren't with me. I'll be back before you know it."

"Sure. I'll just be sitting here doing a cross stitch while you're gone." He frowned. "Fine. I'll give you some money. Get what you think we need."

Brea leaned a hip against the old laminate countertop. "I don't think we should stay here overlong. Maybe lay low for a few days."

"How far is Raúl's place?"

"His home is actually in La Paz. Seeing as how we are just over the border of Mexico, we have over nine hundred miles to cover straight south."

Draven's eyes rounded. "And you made me ditch the car? We sure in the hell can't walk that far."

She laughed. "Relax. He has a vacation home close to the border. Something tells me he's there since he's dead set on finding me. The home is on the coast in Ensenada, which is about sixty to seventy miles. All we need to do is follow 1D and we'll run into it."

"I hope you're speaking figuratively." He took another sip of his coffee. "Still a hell of a long way by foot."

"When I go into town, I'll look for an old beater we might be able to purchase. Enough money down here buys anything." Her gaze fell to his chest again. She needed to get a grip. "Maybe we should both get dressed."

Draven set his mug on the counter and stepped forward. He gripped her chin and tipped her face, forcing her to look at him. "Do I make you uncomfortable?"

"I should probably get going," she whispered, having trouble finding her voice. What she really felt like doing was wrapping her legs around his lean waist and sinking her fangs back into his flesh. Yep, she needed to put lots of space between them. Brea set her mug next to his. "Help yourself to more coffee. Your clothes should be dry by now, so you can get dressed."

She headed for the bathroom, feeling his gaze on her ass as she walked away.

"My wallet is by the faucet. Take what you need."

Brea heard his chuckles as she closed the door behind her and leaned against it. There was a reason Joseph never introduced her to Draven before. No question he would've known on sight Draven was exactly Brea's type. The man made her toes curls every time she was near him. Damn Joseph for setting up their meeting upon his death. Her mate was assuring she'd not be alone.

Tears rolled down her cheeks.

Exactly the kind of selfless act she'd normally expect from him.

CHAPTER FIVE

BREA WALKED INTO COMERCIAL MEXICANA PLAZA RIO IN TI-juana, looking to get Draven some food for the next few days. She might be able to survive on the blood she had ingested for the next three days or so, but he'd need human sustenance. From the cabin it had been a short ten mile run through the woods, only taking her about thirty minutes. Thankfully, she had talked Draven into staying behind. On foot, it would've taken them five or six times as long, if he would have made it at all. Brea spoke fluent Spanish, but she wanted to come across as a tourist rather than draw attention to herself. This close to the border, she was positive most would be well-versed in English.

Gathering a few staples, Brea approached the checkout and laid the items on the counter. "Hello," she said with a smile. "I only have US dollars. Is that going to be a problem?"

"No, *señorita*." The cashier smiled in return. "I can take your money."

"Awesome. Can you also tell me where I might get US currency changed into pesos?"

Moments later and a short jaunt down the block, Brea left the Santander Bank with enough pesos to hopefully secure them a decent ride to Ensenada. Since she didn't want to leave a paper trail for her godfather to pick up on, she needed to find a local willing to part with his vehicle. Three grocery sacks in hand, she walked down a few residential streets, not having much luck. Just as she was coming to the edge of town, Brea spotted a young man sitting on a stoop. An older Triumph motorcycle had been parked in the gravel drive.

Brea walked down the road, noting the man's gaze on her. She turned into his driveway. "*Perdóname*. Do you speak English?"

He placed a hand above his eyes to shield them from the sun as he looked up at her. "*Sí*."

"Is that motorcycle yours?"

"*Sí*." He nodded.

She set her grocery bags down by her feet. "I'd like to buy it from you."

"It's not for sale, *señorita*."

The bike didn't look like it was worth more than a thousand dollars in the US, but she needed transportation with no questions asked. "Does it run?"

"*Sí*."

"I'll give you forty-five thousand pesos."

His eyes lit up, obviously knowing what a deal she had offered him. "*¿Estas loca?*"

She supposed he thought she was a bit on the crazy side to strike such a bargain. "If you have two helmets, I'll give you thirty-five hundred more pesos."

The older bike sported two saddlebags in which to carry her groceries. The transportation would be ideal. No one would be looking for them on a motorcycle and the helmets would help conceal their identity.

"I don't know, *señorita*."

"Fifty thousand pesos and not a peso more."

The young man shook his head and stood, dusting off the seat of his pants. "You have a deal, *señorita*," he said, before walking into the small house and returning with two helmets, each having a dark tinted face shield. He handed her a set of keys.

Perfect.

Brea counted out the pesos and gave them to the man. Thankfully, Draven had the foresight to bring a great deal of cash with them so they could stay under the radar, no matter where they traveled. Brea quickly stowed the sacks of groceries and one of the helmets before slipping her leg over the worn black seat and starting the bike. She thanked the man before strapping on her helmet and circling the drive. Joseph had taught her to ride shortly after they had met, so riding came naturally for her.

Luck had been on her side today. She prayed it held out.

Fifteen minutes later, she pulled the motorcycle down the thin, overgrown lane heading for the cabin. When the small wooden structure came into view, she spotted Draven standing on the porch, hands in his pocket. Apparently, he had heard her arrival long before he spotted her. Brea pulled the bike to a stop, placed both of her feet on the ground, and cut the engine.

She took off her helmet and grinned. "Check out our new ride."

He took the two steps down from the small front porch and walked over to her. "Not bad for short notice. Where did you find it?"

"I paid a young man handsomely for it. No title, just cash. It can't be traced."

"He saw you."

Brea shrugged. "It couldn't be helped. Let's hope he's forgetful if my godfather's goons come around. What are you doing out here? I could've been one of the gunmen."

"You could have." Though he didn't look concerned in the least. He shrugged. "I saw the bike through the trees on the bend in the lane, long before you spotted me. You weren't big enough to be one of those goons."

She kicked down the side stand and stepped over the bike, placing the helmet on the seat. "You can't be too safe, Draven. These men aren't to be toyed with. You need to take them seriously."

"You forget I was the one shot at." His face sobered. "I don't think I'm making light of it."

"I haven't forgotten." She walked up to him and moved the shoulder of his shirt to the side, seeing the wound was healing without infection. "Can you get the groceries from the saddlebags?"

Brea walked into the house and headed for the kitchen, trying her damnedest to get a hold of her emotions. Draven was trying to play down what had happened yesterday, but it still rankled her ire. He could've been killed, and all because he had the misfortune of being tangled up in her mess. Another thing she would see her godfather pay for. He had no right to interfere in her life. And even less of a right to kill Joseph.

She wouldn't give Raúl the opportunity to hurt Draven, even if it meant leaving him behind … even if it meant sacrificing her own life. Draven's reasoning for going with her had been two-fold. Being there for her was only part of it, she knew running from the Devils had been the other part. Draven had been instrumental in bringing them down. And with his help, the DEA had arrested several key members, thus putting a target on his back with the MC.

"Where do you want these?"

She pointed to the cupboard next to her. "I couldn't get anything that needed to be kept refrigerated. I hope it's suitable."

He pulled out a jar of peanut butter, a loaf of bread, six bottles of water, some fruit, and a few bags of snacks. "Junk food?"

"The peanut butter is protein." She turned, leaning her hip against the laminate, and smiled. "I haven't had to buy real food in a very long time. Besides, I had no idea what you'd like. I figured everyone liked peanut butter."

"Not if I have allergies."

Her gaze widened. "Oh my gosh. I'm sorry. I hadn't—"

"Relax, I'm only kidding." Draven had a boyish charm to his smile. Brea found she quite liked it. "Peanut butter sandwiches will work just fine, even if I would prefer a perfectly grilled steak. I realize, out here in the middle of Timbuktu, that wouldn't be very practical."

"I promise you, I'll take you out for a real steak dinner when this is all over."

His gaze sobered. "Like a date?"

Brea's heart skipped a beat. The thought of going on an actual date with Draven had the butterflies fluttering in her stomach, something she hadn't felt in a long time. Her gaze dropped to the floor, wishing for normality.

She had begged Joseph for immortality and he had obliged. Now she understood his hesitation. Being a vampire had its drawbacks. Brea could date, she supposed, but falling in love with a human wouldn't be ideal. While she would live forever, whoever her heart stupidly fell for would eventually grow old and die. She already had one heartbreak. She didn't want to go through it all again.

A date?

They were better off keeping things platonic. When this whole mess was over, she could disappear without her heart dying a little bit for leaving him behind. And she would leave. Her life belonged to her. The Sons of Sangue and their rules about unmated females be damned.

"Sorry," Draven apologized, bringing her attention back to their conversation. "I didn't mean to assume."

"I'm the one who is sorry, Draven." She walked over to him and laid her hand against his cheek. "I should've never involved you, or led you to believe this could be anything more. You're a good man."

Draven stepped back from her touch, sending gooseflesh skittering down her flesh from the sudden iciness of his gaze. She shivered.

"Thanks for the food."

Draven turned his back on her, opened a few drawers, and found a butter knife, then began making himself a sandwich. He grabbed one of the water bottles and headed for the front of the cabin. The door slapped loudly behind him, causing her to jump. Brea watched him through the screen take a seat on an old wooden rocker, staring into the distance as he took a large bite out of his sandwich and chewed.

How could she have been so thoughtless? After all, he had given up for her.

Brea took a deep breath and headed for the bathroom. Maybe a shower would help her clear her mind. Stopping in front of the cracked mirror over the sink, she took a good long look at the woman staring back at her, hating what she saw.

A bitter, selfish woman.

CHAPTER SIX

DRAVEN STARED INTO THE DISTANCE AND TOOK ANOTHER bite of his sandwich. *Peanut butter.* Not that he didn't like the spread, but he was more of a meat kind of guy. Popping the last bit of sandwich into his mouth, he dusted off his hands on his jeans. He was a selfish bastard. What the hell had he been thinking in there? He wasn't here to date Brea, for God's sake.

A date? Seriously? What were they? In high school?

Birds chirped, their wings fluttering through the leaves, drawing his attention to the foliage. A black hawk perched on a nearby branch before taking flight, his wing span massive. He envied the bird's freedom, something he had given up the minute he had agreed to work with the DEA. Once he returned to Oregon, the Devils would have him on their hit list, no two ways about it. And the MC who could possibly help him, he had hidden a huge secret from—Joseph Sala's mate.

If he were smart, which he wasn't since he was allowing Brea to lead him around by his fucking balls, he would've taken off, gone overseas, and stayed with friends. Instead, he sat here in the back fucking forty, eating a peanut butter sandwich, and sharing a tiny cottage with a woman who teased his libido with the simple scent of her flesh.

When this was over, and he saw Brea through this crazy notion to visit her godfather, then he ought to think seriously about moving far away. At least until this damn ordeal blew over and all his enemies forgot about him. The Devils and the Sons of Sangue couldn't hold grudges forever. He shook his head and let out a weary sigh. They were both MCs, for crying out loud. Of course, they did.

Technically, the Sons didn't even know about Brea, but it was only a matter of time. They had a mutual enemy. Once they found out about her, and the fact he had kept her confidential, his favor with the Sons would come to an end. He may provide them with donors, but truthfully, anyone willing to keep their secret could do as much.

Finishing off his bottle of water, setting the empty next to the leg of the chair, he stood and stepped from the porch, heading down the dirt path leading to the cabin. He needed to clear his head, and that wasn't going to happen with Brea so close in proximity. Not when he wanted to fuck her in the worst way.

Joseph had been one lucky son of a bitch.

If he allowed himself, Draven could easily see himself falling for the sprite. He had dated and screwed his way through half of Florence, and none of them had captivated him the way she did. It was as if she had cast some ridiculous spell over him, one that had him thinking of very little other than what she'd feel like from the inside. He wanted to take his time, strip her slow, and lick every soft inch of her flesh until he knew all there was to know about her.

Joseph.

Draven swore up a blue streak as he pushed his long bangs from his face. Thinking of Joseph sliding between her slender legs was a huge buzz kill. Maybe that could be his new line of defense. Every time his libido went off the charts, he'd picture Joseph's ugly mug between her slender thighs.

He hadn't exactly been one of the better looking Sons of Sangue members, like Alexander. That man had the face of a freaking model. Him he could understand. But Joseph? It was either the man's good nature Brea had been drawn to or he had one hell of a big cock.

It wasn't long before his trek through the woods, and off the beaten path, before he found himself back at the cabin, staring at the backside of the small wooden structure. Draven wasn't ready to make his way indoors, not knowing if Brea had finished with her shower. He had wanted to give her space, not have her worry about his dumb ass trying to sneak a peek.

Movement in the window drew his attention. Brea passed by the dirty panes, sans clothing. *Fuck me!* She stopped, her head bent over the sink beneath the cracked glass. Her small but perky breasts were in full view, her light pink nipples begging to be drawn between his lips. His mouth went dry and his cock sprung to life. Draven was frozen to the ground, staring at the gorgeous nymph before him.

Brea glanced up, her baby blues locking on his, her water bottle paused halfway to her lips. Just fucking wonderful. Now he looked like a goddamn Peeping Tom. He quickly averted his gaze, then made a beeline for the front of the cabin. Heat rose up his neck, shaming him. Draven retook his seat on the porch, afraid to go inside and confront her. What the hell would he say? He shook his head and leaned forward, bracing his forearms on his knees. Normally, he wouldn't have given two shits what a woman thought of his ogling. He had eyes and he damn well knew how to use them.

Brea was different.

Her opinion of him mattered.

Joseph had handed her over to his care and he was doing a bang-up job so far. If the vampire could see how he was taking care of his mate, he'd think again about his decision. Draven was the last person Joseph should've entrusted her care to.

The screen door's rusty hinges creaked, alerting him to the fact Brea had joined him. A quick glance back proved as much. She stood stationary, now fully clothed, apparently unsure what to say herself. At least she wasn't reading him the riot act, even if he did deserve it. The image of her tits was burned against the back of his eyelids. They may have been small, but they had been perfect.

The wood creaked beneath her footfalls. Brea pulled a chair from the back of the porch, the legs screeching against the decking, then took a seat. A small wooden box, upturned for a makeshift table, was the only thing separating them. She set a water bottle on the surface next to him. "Sorry. I guess I should've thought to buy you something with a little more kick than water."

Draven trained his gaze back to the forest. "It's fine. Even if I could use a whiskey right about now."

"Draven?"

"What?"

"Look at me."

He did as she asked. Instead of the anger he expected, Draven saw something else in her gaze, something close to sorrow.

"I'm not unaffected, you know."

Sitting back in the chair, he crossed his legs at the ankles. "I'm sorry. I wasn't—"

"It's okay." She smiled, her cheeks reddening. "Don't think I didn't wonder what you would've looked like without that towel wrapping your waist."

He groaned. "Don't do this, Brea. I'm so fucking attracted to you. I'm not sure how much more restraint I have. Knowing you're interested, makes me want you more."

She drew her lower lip between her teeth, her gaze never leaving his. Finally, she said, "Am I bad person?"

His brows drew together. "What in the hell would make you think that?"

"Joseph hasn't been gone long. Yet, all I can think of is my desire to know you more."

"Can I ask you a question?"

She nodded, her hands clasped tightly in her lap, whitening her knuckles.

Knowing vampires were sexual beings, he couldn't help his curiosity. "You mentioned that you hadn't had sex with Joseph for a month before his death. Why?"

She took in a shuddering breath before looking into the distance. "I loved Joseph. Deeply. We had been together for a long time. He gave me my immortality. I begged him to make me his mate. He treated me like a princess most times."

"Most times?"

Brea looked back at him, the sorrow still written in her gaze. "In the beginning, everything was great. But toward the end, I think he regretted saddling himself with me. He'd go to the Rave, hang with the guys more often. When he'd come home, he wouldn't even talk to me. I brushed it off as moodiness. One day, he brought home a couple of donors. It wasn't anything new because he made sure I was fed, taken care of. It was important to keep me hidden from the Sons because of my godfather, as you know."

Draven nodded. He had seen Joseph leave quite often with a donor on each arm.

"A little over a month ago was no different. He brought home two donors. One was very pretty ...gorgeous, in fact. Long, dark brown hair. The exact opposite of me. I tried not to be jealous as he sank his fangs into her neck. I did the same to my donor."

A tear rolled down her cheek. "When we finished feeding, usually he would send them both on their way. Not this time. He fucked his donor right in front of me. Fucked her while I watched, Draven. He died a little over a month later. We never talked after what he did, nor did I make love to him again."

CHAPTER SEVEN

WELL, THAT CERTAINLY CHANGED THINGS.

If Joseph hadn't respected Brea in the end, then Draven didn't feel the need to honor the fact they had been mated. Brea obviously mourned her mate's loss. After all, she had said she loved Joseph. Her feelings for him hadn't shut off because he had become a first class ass. Out of reverence for her, he'd give her time to come to terms with the loss. Draven wasn't a complete, unfeeling fuck. But the gloves were off and it was only a matter of time before he would give in to the desire running rampant through him. His dick twitched at the prospect. Damn thing would have to acknowledge his change of heart.

"What the hell?" Draven rubbed his jaw, still stunned by her admission. "I don't even know what to say, other than apologize for him since he's too dead to do it himself. What an ass-wipe. He didn't deserve you, Brea."

Using her palms, she wiped the wetness from her cheeks. A nervous chuckle escaped her. "I spent the last few years trying to convince myself that I deserved Kinky. His last cruel act was not like him at all. I think that's why I was so blind-sided by what he did. I was left wondering what I had done. But since he wasn't talking to me, I couldn't even ask."

Draven had to know. "Had you led him to believe that there was someone else?"

"Are you serious?" Her blue gaze heated. "I would never have harmed Kinky in any way. That is such a guy thing to say."

"I am a guy." He chuckled. "I'm having a hard time wrapping my head around the fact Kinky fucked a donor right in front of you. He cared about you enough to send you my way should something happen. To me, that shows he wanted you protected. So why the hell would he be so callous?"

She worried her lower lip. "I guess we'll never know now."

He resisted the urge to pull her onto his lap and hold her, even if his intentions were nothing more than comfort. Taking advantage of the situation wasn't his style, and he didn't want Brea thinking it was.

"So what's our plan from here?" Draven asked, looking for a change in subjects. They had dwelled enough on Joseph's infidelity. "As much as I'd like to lie low here for a while, it's only a matter of time before Raúl's men find us."

"You're probably right. We need to keep you safe."

Draven shook his head. He really hated being the weak one in the relationship. "I'd like to argue my case, but I know it's a moot point. They come gunning for us, I'm the one who has to fear getting his ass shot off and joining Kinky... Jesus, that was insensitive."

He couldn't stay off the topic even when he tried. The fact anyone could not remain faithful to this woman blew him away. If he couldn't do it, then he wasn't the right man for her either. She deserved better than being someone's fuck buddy.

"Don't worry about it, Draven. It is what it is. I can't stay mad at the dead forever. Kinky deserves forgiveness as much as anyone else. I may not have understood it, but I forgave him."

She licked her lips, drawing his attention to them again. "As far as where we go from here, I say we head straight for Ensenada. It's about a little over an hour from here by motorcycle. I say we hang here for a few more days, give them a reason to spread out among the countryside, leaving few behind with Raúl. Better for us. We go marching in there with all his men present and neither of us stands a chance."

"I still think you're crazy. It's a suicide mission."

"Promise me, Draven, if things get hairy—leave me."

He took in a deep breath, then sighed heavily. Not happening. "Like hell, I will. What kind of a man do you take me for?"

"A live one." Brea placed her hand on his knee, then quickly removed it as if stung from the contact. "I don't want your death on me too. It's bad enough I feel responsible for Kinky."

"Even if you're correct, and Raúl put the hit out on him, you're not to be blamed for that. The man is a psycho. He's responsible for thousands of deaths in Mexico alone. Kinky was just another number for him."

"And I won't allow you to be a number. This isn't up for discussion. You either promise to get the hell out of there if things get dicey, or I'll leave your ass behind now."

"Why do you care what happens to me? You don't really know me."

"Kinky did. And he thought enough of you to put me in your care."

"A lot of good I would do," he grumbled.

"Exactly." She turned in her chair to face him, tucking her legs beneath her. "Promise me you will leave me if I tell you to."

No way in hell could he give her his word. Instead, he lied. "I'll do what you ask."

Her blue gaze studied him a moment before answering. "Good. We'll leave in a few days."

All Draven could think of was a few long days of nothing to do to pass the time. Oh, he knew what his dick wanted to do. *Again, not happening.* Draven was going to have to get creative at staying busy, or start taking some very long hikes. With his luck, he'd wind up lost and Brea would be forced to come rescue his ass. Draven was not going to come out of this thing with his dignity intact. He might as well hand over that man card now.

CHAPTER EIGHT

TWENTY-FOUR HOURS HAD PASSED SINCE HER CONVERSA-tion with Draven. Following their chat, he had avoided her and barely spoke to her in passing. Brea couldn't help but wonder what she might've done to be on the receiving end of his cold shoulder. Before she had divulged the story about Joseph and the donor, Draven hadn't been shy about his desire. Now she might as well have the plague. Honestly, she didn't think her ego could take another blow.

What the hell was wrong with her DNA?

She sighed. *Other than the family she had been born into.*

Or maybe, with Draven, it was her vampire side he was warring against.

It was certainly possible that Draven regretted following her, offering her protection he was ill equipped for. The odds of surviving gunfire aimed in their direction was definitely in her favor. She stood on the porch and glanced at the motor-cycle hidden in the brush, just off the beaten path and barely visible. A little over seventy miles stood between her and Ensenada. Raúl had to know she was still in the area, maybe even suspected she headed his way. Never a coward, he'd wait for her confrontation, not that he'd feel guilty over Joseph's death. No, Raúl more than likely felt justified if he was the guilty party. He always did.

49

Brea wanted her answers, one way or the other, no matter the tactics. She didn't fear her godfather. Regardless if he was guilty of Joseph's death, he still thought of her as family. He would justify his actions out of love for her. Joseph would've never been good enough for her, neither would Draven.

Which was why, after sunset and Draven had fallen asleep, Brea was going to get on the back of the bike and leave him behind. She couldn't allow him to continue on this fool's mission with her. He had been correct about one thing, for him it would be a suicide mission. Raúl might not harm her, but he had no such loyalty to Draven. If he continued to accompany her, he wouldn't make it out alive. Brea cared too much for the barkeep to allow any harm to come to him.

She couldn't repay his kindness by pitting him against a cold-hearted kingpin.

Decision made, she made to enter the cabin. The screen door swung out, startling her, and Draven walked through as though her thoughts had conjured him up. He looked good enough to...What? Most definitely drink from. The familiar ache began in her gums. Feeding before she headed out was a must. She couldn't go up against her godfather weak from the lack of nourishment. The problem was that she wasn't so sure Draven would be of the giving mind.

"What?" he asked, eyeing her skeptically.

"Nothing." Brea clasped her hands behind her and rocked back on her heels.

"Then why are you looking at me that way?"

She ran her tongue over lips, hoping to sooth away the impending lengthening of her fangs. "I was just about to go inside."

"And look for me?"

"Why would I do that? You've hardly talked to me."

Draven rubbed his neck. "Look, I've been unfair."

"For the life of me, Draven, I can't figure out what I've done to piss you off."

His gaze widened. "Is that what you think?"

"What else am I to think? We're stuck in this small cabin, and we can't help be in each other's company, yet you seem to be doing your damnedest to avoid being anywhere near me."

He gripped her shoulders, pulling her within inches of him. She could smell his woodsy scent, intoxicating her. Her eyes heated as their black vampire state threatened to take over. This close, she had one hell of a time denying her desire, or her hunger.

"God, Brea, I'm avoiding you because I want to fuck the shit out of you."

Her breath hitched and her fangs punched from her gums. Damn her weak hide.

"I feel like a walking erection around you and there isn't a damn thing I'm willing to do about it."

"Why?" she whispered. "Why won't you take what I would willingly offer?"

He let go of her, stepped back, and took a deep steadying breath. "You came to me not that long ago, devastated when you found out what had happened to Kinky."

"Because I loved him."

"Exactly. I'm not about to sully that love by being your pity fuck."

"Is that what you think?"

Draven jammed a hand through his hair. "Not only that, but I find out Kinky wasn't even deserving of that love."

A fat tear slipped from her lash and rolled down her cheek. "But he was. He took me in… He gave me immortality because I begged him to. Don't you get it, Draven? I *forced* myself onto him. Not the other way around. I took away his choice. I was the reason he found himself mated. He didn't choose me. How could I be mad when I decided for him?"

"You're cutting yourself short."

"Maybe. But how would you feel if you suddenly found yourself stuck with me?"

Draven opened his mouth to speak, then just as quickly closed it. *Exactly.* What man would want to find themselves in an instant relationship with no out? Marriages had divorce. Mating was for life.

Brea wiped away the wetness from her cheek. "You don't know my and Kinky's relationship. You don't know what he had to endure because of me. I was the selfish one. Not him. I took what I wanted."

One of Draven's brows arched up. "Are you telling me you took Kinky's blood, that he didn't offer it to you?"

She shook her head, looking at her bare feet. She ran her toes along one of the boards. "I would've never taken that without his permission."

"Then you weren't in that relationship solely because you were selfish. Kinky agreed to it. He may have later regretted his hasty decision—"

"He was fucking me, Draven." She choked on a sob. "I waited until he was deep inside me for the first time. I waited until he was so far gone in lust that he would have done anything I asked. That's when I begged him."

"And did he hesitate?"

"Yes." More tears slipped from her lashes. "Goddamn it, yes. He stilled inside of me, holding himself back. And when I said, 'If you ever cared about me, then you would protect me with your blood.' Don't you get it? Yes, I loved Kinky. But even more than that, I wanted the strength he had. I never wanted to be a victim or to be afraid of my godfather. I used his desire against him to get what I wanted. He presented me with an opportunity to be much stronger than Raúl Trevino Caballero or any of his henchmen. I was the last of my family and I knew it was only a matter of time before he tried to claim me."

She glanced back up. "I thought if I was already taken, then Raúl would give up and leave me be."

"What exactly did Raúl want from you?" He drew the words out slowly.

"He wants me for his own, Draven. It's why he's so adamant in getting me back. He wants me for his bride."

CHAPTER NINE

SPEECHLESS. WHAT THE HELL WAS HE SUPPOSED TO SAY TO that?

Draven was pretty sure Raúl Trevino Caballero was used to getting what he wanted. Right now, apparently that was Brea. The old pervert had to be at least twice her age. He rubbed his jaw, watching the vampire part of her retreat. Her rising desire, hunger, or whatever had her about to unleash her vampy DNA, had quickly receded with the confession of her godfather wanting her in the biblical sense.

Okay, just nasty.

Regardless of the fact that he's a short, fat troll ... he's a fucking monster.

Draven would've gladly offered up his own single status if he thought marrying her might be the answer. But the only thing he'd accomplish by getting hitched to Brea would be him following Joseph to an early grave. Hell, he wasn't too sure he wouldn't wind up six-feet under anyway. Raúl's goons had already tried their damnedest to put a bullet in him.

"Say something, Draven."

"What the hell am I supposed to say to that? It might've been helpful to know that from the start, Brea."

Her head jerked as if he had physically slapped her. It had been a low blow, even coming from his smart ass. Had he the prior knowledge, he still wouldn't have allowed her to go on the fool's mission alone. Like it or not, they were stuck with each other, seeing this objective through to the end. Draven prayed he'd be alive long enough to see Brea exact her revenge. If he were to die, then he wanted to make damn sure he took Raúl with him. If anyone deserved a quick trip to hell, it was her godfather.

"You can leave anytime you want, Draven." Her gaze narrowed. *Yep, he had pissed her off.* "No one is stopping you. As a matter of fact, I'd prefer you leave. You'd just get in my way anyway. If you go with me, then I have to worry about saving your sorry ass."

"Jesus! Chill the hell out, Brea." He scrubbed his hand down his slightly whiskered jaw. "I didn't mean I wouldn't be here for you. I'm sorry, but Raúl wanting you for his wife took me a bit by surprise."

"Well, that makes two of us." Her breath shuttered out of her. "Let me tell you, that will never happen. I'll see him dead first. Out of respect for who Raúl was to me, I thought mating with Joseph was the best option. I did love Joseph, so it seemed like the perfect solution. I had no idea Raúl would kill him. I can't be responsible for your death too. I was serious when I said I preferred that you leave. It's the only way I can protect you."

He stepped forward, framing her face with his palms. "What kind of man would I be if I left you to face that monster alone?"

"A live one."

His gaze dropped to her bow-shaped lips. Kissing her was a bad idea. *A really, really bad idea.* And yet, he couldn't stop the flash flood of emotion running through his veins. He wanted to taste her, feel her soft lips against his. He slid the pad of his thumb over her lower lip. Her eyes darkened to endless, black pools. Draven's own desire reflected back at him from the mirror-like surface. Her shoulders squared, telling him she warred with denying him the caress. No matter how hard she tried, her vampire DNA still emerged, telling him she wanted the same thing.

Draven took a tentative step forward, giving her time to formulate the word "no" if she chose. Brea's lips parted. Slipping one hand around her neck and up the back of her skull, he tilted her face. Still, she remained silent. Her pink tongue darted out, wetting the seal of her mouth.

One simple taste.

He lowered his head and kissed her. Just a touch, a slight meeting of flesh. Draven might have stopped there, but her gasp had him slanting his lips and slipping his tongue into the soft cavern of her mouth. The tentative touch of her tongue to his elicited a groan from him.

She slipped her hands under his tee, over his flesh and stopped on his pecs. His cock took notice, his jeans becoming uncomfortable and far too tight. Draven suddenly wished for the towel that had once been draping his waist. The fucking rough material of his pants was far too constraining. His balls needed space and his cock wanted freedom.

Brea slid her fingernails down his flesh, sending gooseflesh popping out in their wake, down his chest to abs, stopping just above the waistband of his jeans. Lord, he prayed she didn't back out now. He wanted nothing more than to shed his clothes and sink deeply inside her. His erection lengthened at the prospect of driving home.

Home.

Something told Draven if he ever allowed himself to make love to her, that's exactly what it would feel like. Like going home.

She broke the kiss and looked at him. "Draven?"

Her tone was quiet, so much so, he almost didn't hear her over his pulse pounding in his ears. *Please, for the love of all that's holy, don't back out now.* He raised his gaze to hers, taking in a deep breath and lowering his hands to his sides. Draven ran his damp palms against the rough denim.

"What do you need, sweetheart?"

"I need to feed."

He bit back a curse. "Of course, you do."

Disappointment sluiced through him. Had her response to him been nothing more than her need to feed? How the hell could he be so wrong at reading the signs? He let out a long deep sigh, resigning himself to another day of blue balls.

He wasn't sure how long they could hole up in the small cabin, or how long they would continue to be safe there. Time was not on their side. It wouldn't be long before Raúl's men combed the countryside and happened upon them. She'd need to feed so they could take the motorcycle and head for Ensenada. Draven refused, however, to ride behind her, no matter how well she knew how to ride. She had taken enough of his manhood on this trip.

"One condition."

One of her delicate brows raised. "A condition for you to feed me?"

He nodded. "When we leave here, I drive."

A slow smile grew on her lips, before becoming a full-blown laugh. She wiped a tear from the corner of her eyes. "You can drive, Draven."

"Thank you." He returned her humor with a smile of his own. "Let's take it inside. If you cause me to faint, I'd hate to embarrass myself out here. Besides, the wood flooring doesn't look like a soft landing."

Her eyes twinkled in merriment. "You've not fainted once when I drank from you."

"There's a first time for everything."

He turned and entered the house, not bothering to wait for her. If she wanted to feed, she'd damn well follow. Like it or not, her rejection stung. Sleeping with Brea was wrong on so many levels, and yet he couldn't stop from hungering for her, any more than he could his desire to protect her. No matter if her vampire genes made her stronger, Draven was a man. And as such, it was his nature to want to keep her safe.

The screen door slapped behind him. Draven sank to the floor in front of the worn sofa, putting himself on her level. Brea walked over to him and sat on the sofa, her razor-sharp fangs visible beneath her upper lip. A shiver racked his spine. He doubted he'd ever get used to offering up his blood, or the sight of her vampy side. She was menacing looking to be sure, but one huge fucking turn-on nonetheless.

Her scent wafted to his nose, further hardening his dick. He wanted her in a really bad way, even before she sank her fangs deep into his neck. Draven couldn't imagine how much more his libido could take. He was afraid the minute she sank her fangs gum-deep and applied the suction, he'd embarrass himself. It was either that or he was going to have the sorest set of balls to date.

CHAPTER TEN

ER FANGS PIERCED HIS FLESH WITH A SOFT POP. EUPHORIA traveled through his veins. There was no other way to explain the extreme calm, mixed with the intense pleasure, that washed over him. His hardened dick pained him. And damn him for desiring it all. He wanted Brea suckling his neck while he drove his cock balls-deep into her. Pumping his hips, tightening his ass muscles, slamming into her until they both reached their climax. No doubt about it. It would be epic.

And he hated himself for wanting it.

Draven was so fucking close to tossing Brea on her back and stripping away her pants, taking his deepest desire. The only thing stopping him…

Fuck!

The bastard didn't even deserve the respect. He had screwed a donor in front of Brea. Holding back from acting on his hunger was no longer about revering Joseph. Hell, no. He no longer respected the dead vampire. It was out of his deep regard for Brea. Her decisions in life had always been governed by others, even her determination to mate with Joseph. Brea might think she took away Joseph's choice to find a mate of his choosing, but the biker had a voice. Draven was pretty sure *no* was part of his vocabulary. His decision to mate with her was surely driven by lust. Had Joseph been in love with her, Draven was pretty sure he would've followed Brea through hell and back, not fucked a donor in front of her.

Draven couldn't pretend to know what Joseph had been thinking, but his actions weren't motivated out of love. Not that Draven was an expert on the subject, but he would've never treated Brea so crassly, not to mention he'd follow her through hell and back if need be.

Love.

The word floated around his brain like a taunt. *Oh, fuck no!* How the hell had the emotion sneaked up on him? Draven's chest swelled. There must've been a damn Cupid hiding somewhere in the godforsaken woods, who had crept up on him from behind and shot him straight through the back. *The fucking coward.* Draven was pretty sure before he got here that four letter word wasn't even a blip on his radar.

Brea released her fangs from his neck. The soft pad of her tongue slipped over the twin puncture wounds, sealing them with her saliva. Within hours, they would no longer be visible, another product of her vampire genes.

Her hands on his shoulders, she pushed back from him and leaned against the sofa. Brea dropped her hold and released a shaky sigh as he glanced back at her. Moisture pooled in her eyes and her lower lip trembled.

The swelling in his chest quickly turned to an ache. The sadness he saw in her expression affected him as deeply as the realization he loved her. The question was what the hell was he going to do about it? Draven supposed he could ignore it, push it aside and try like hell to pretend it didn't exist.

Or he could follow her all the way to Ensenada, undoubtedly getting himself killed in the process.

Unless…

Oh, hell no!

He couldn't.

Once the plan began to formulate, there was no shaking it. It was the only answer. He'd protect her with his life. But as it was, against the cartel and her uncle, he was about as useless as a gnat. Draven knew Brea would never agree to it, knew she might even hate him for it. He had no other choice but to seduce her. She wouldn't know of his scheme until it was far too late for her to do anything about it.

"You going to be okay, sweetheart?"

"I can't have you go through with this, Draven."

"With?"

"Going to Ensenada. I've made up my mind and nothing you say will change that." She wiped away a stray tear. "You won't survive, and I can't see you dead too."

"You're leaving me behind? When did you decide this?"

"A little while ago." She leaned forward and gripped his hand, intertwining their fingers. "I intended on leaving when you fell asleep."

"So why tell me now?"

"Because you deserve better than me sneaking out in the wee hours. I don't want you thinking I thought you a coward or weak. I wanted you to know that I believe you are one hell of a good man to come with me this far."

She looked down at her lap briefly. When she gazed back up, he could see the hatred in her eyes. "I originally tried to protect my godfather, thinking he at least deserved that from the love he had shown me while I was growing up. His wanting me for his wife was beside the point. I figured mating with Kinky, he'd let go of the silly notion. Instead, I find out he most likely orchestrated his death. Kinky might've been a complete jerk in the end, whatever his reasoning, I will never know why. But I did love him regardless, and Raúl needs to be punished if he's indeed the guilty party."

Draven squeezed her fingers. "You?"

"Who else?" She let go of him, sat back, drew her legs to her chest, and hugged her knees. "No one can get as close as I can. And if I show up dragging you along, I won't have a chance in hell getting on the inside either. I have to go it alone."

"And if he decides to kill you?"

"He won't."

"You don't know that, Brea." Draven couldn't keep the anger from his tone. Raúl was not a man to be trusted. "I can't let you go alone."

"And I won't let you go with me. Don't make me hypnotize you into staying put."

His ire skyrocketed, heat rising up his neck. Draven would be damned if he'd allow her to take away his free choice, making him even more determined to push through with his plan. "Fine."

"That easy?" Brea's gaze narrowed. "What are you up to, Draven?"

"You said it yourself, I'm no match for your godfather, and you have a better chance getting inside without me."

She nodded, still eyeing him cautiously.

"I will agree on one condition."

"Man, you're all about conditions. First, you want to drive. Now?"

Draven chuckled. "What can I say? You force me to bargain in order to get what I want."

Leaning forward, Brea ran a hand along his whiskered jaw. "What can I possibly give you, Draven?"

"Make love to me."

Brea sat back, her gaze widened. "I'm not sure—"

"You're going off to meet the devil himself. I don't even know if you'll be coming back. Can you promise me you will?"

"I wish I could. But I'm walking into the unknown. I may be stronger and harder to kill, but that doesn't mean that I can't be."

Draven stood, pulling her to her feet. He framed her face, staring into her beautiful dark gaze. This had to work. If it didn't, she'd not likely ever talk to him again. Slanting his lips over hers, he kissed her deeply, possessively. When he was finished, she'd be his in every sense of the word. There would be no turning back.

Brea fisted his shirt, kissing him with fervor. She tasted of his own blood, almost making him change his mind about moving forward with his intention. But as she leaned in and her abdomen rested against the steel length of him, he knew what he had to do.

He broke the kiss, resting his forehead against hers. His breath sawed out of him as if he had already run a marathon. He was nervous and excited. Making love to Brea was all he had thought about the past few days.

"Brea," he breathed out.

"Yes?"

"Make love to me."

She slid her small hands up his chest, searing his flesh as her palms smoothed over him. Her fingers intertwined in the hair at his nape. Pulling him forward, she kissed him, her tongue slipping past his lips and teasing his into a response.

Draven had his answer.

Reaching down, he slipped an arm beneath her knees and picked her up, heading for the small bed. She broke the kiss, her gaze seeking his.

"Sweetheart, I'm going to fuck you senseless."

Brea shook her head, damn near causing his heart to stop beating. A smile grew on her lips. "You said make love, Draven. I'm holding you to that."

Draven chuckled, feeling more light-hearted than he had a right to. He was about to trick her, even though it was for her own damn good. And he intended on enjoying every fucking minute of it.

CHAPTER ELEVEN

THIS WAS A BAD IDEA ON SO MANY LEVELS. *TELL THAT TO her vampire genes, which were screaming to get laid.* Joseph had left her ego in tatters. Brea might not have mated with him for the right reason, but she had loved him nonetheless. To watch him make love to the donor had been like a knife to her heart. She swore she'd never love again. The pain had been too raw, damn near crushing her. Brea had become a blubbering mess whenever Joseph had gone off to the Blood 'n' Rave. In truth, she had mourned his loss long before his death.

His ghost didn't deserve to be in this room with Draven.

Brea glanced up from the middle of the bed, her gaze raking Draven from head to toe, and all thoughts of Joseph evaporated. Draven looked more delicious than the day he traipsed around in nothing but the white terry cloth towel. She knew, cartel be damned, Draven would never allow her to go to Ensenada alone. He had left behind his beloved car and traipsed through miles of dense foliage, all the while being shot at, some of the bullets grazing his flesh.

And yet, here he stood.

Draven didn't fool her. He wasn't about to let her go off to meet her godfather on her own. His spoken fine hadn't convinced her. So what was his angle? Did he think by making love to her that she might fall for him, ensuring she wouldn't dare leave him behind? Too late. It was the exact reason she was leaving him behind. Draven Smith had captured a piece of her heart, cockiness and all. As a matter of fact, she found that particular part quite endearing.

"You going to stand there all day, barkeep?"

His slow smile robbed her of breath. He reached for the hem of his shirt and pulled it over his head, tossing it to the floor. Draven wasn't overly muscled, more like that of a fitness trainer. Tall, lean muscled, and just the right amount of hair sprinkling his pecs. Her gaze followed the dark hair down to his navel, where it circled before aiming straight south, disappearing into the waistband of his jeans. His flesh was free off tattoos. She didn't know why, it wasn't as if she had a thing against skin art, but Brea found she liked his clean skin.

Her gaze moved back up his chest.

A delicious ache started in her lower abdomen at the thought of tugging on his small nipples with her teeth, nipping them before smoothing away the ache with the flat of her tongue. Brea couldn't help wonder what he thought of her multiple piercings, the most notable being her Fourchette Piercing, a small ring at the rear of the vulva. She couldn't help but wonder what he'd think when he... *Oh, please let him be into oral.*

Brea took in a shaky breath, realizing she needed to quiet her thoughts. Her nerves were starting to get the better of her. She was pretty sure Draven would leave a mark when she walked out if his life. If he thought to stop her, she'd be forced to hypnotize his stubborn ass. Brea would be heading for Ensenada … alone.

But first, she intended on loving every sexy inch of him.

"What's on your mind, sweetheart? Second thoughts?"

Rising to her knees, she crawled to the side of the bed and slipped from the tattered mattress to the floor. Draven growled as she knelt at his feet, the sound smoothing over her like a lover's hand. Tucking her tongue into the corner of her lips, she worked the zipper of his jeans. Her gaze took in his. His Adam's apple bobbed. The dark brown of his gaze deepened. The naked desire she saw staring down at her nearly undid her. Draven wanted her, and not because she had her fangs buried deep into his carotid.

"Brea…"

Ignoring the whispered plea, she slipped a hand inside his jeans and encompassed him.

He hissed, gritting his teeth. "You're going to fucking unman me yet."

Pulling his erection from his briefs, another stainless steel ring greeted her. A Prince Albert slipped through the head of his penis. Draven was certainly full of pleasant surprises. Her fangs punched through her gums. Thank goodness she had already fed. The thought of mounting him while suckling the dark, fruity essence of his blood was enticing, but not something she could allow. The loss of too many red blood cells could throw him into anemic shock. He couldn't replenish his blood supply like a vampire could.

Humans were delicate.

A drop of precum leaked from the crown of his erection. Brea licked the small droplet, before taking him into her mouth. She was careful not to scrape her fangs along the silky flesh. One of his hands fisted the hair at the top of her head, guiding him more fully into her mouth. His hips moved rhythmically, earning her another groan. She smoothed her tongue along the bottom side of the shaft as her hand encompassed him.

A shiver shook his body just before his grip tightened in her hair and he forced her to release him. "Not like this, sweetheart."

"You weren't enjoying—"

He pulled her to her feet and slanted his lips over hers, kissing her full of passion and promise. She clung to him and kissed him back, her tongue tangling with his in desperation. Once she left him behind, Brea couldn't be sure she'd ever see him again. Even if she wasn't killed in her mission to take out her godfather, she'd be forced to go into hiding. Should she manage to kill Raúl, the La Paz cartel wouldn't stop until they saw her dead. Brea couldn't ask Draven to give up any more than he already had.

He stepped back from her, breaking the kiss. Gripping the edge of her top, he pulled it over her head, and tossed it with his onto the floor. Brea pushed her pants and panties over her hips and stepped out of them. Her bra went next, leaving her standing naked and vulnerable. Draven smoothed a knuckle over her cheek before running the digit slowly down her neck. He opened his hand and ran the back of it over her soft flesh, brushing the steel ring in one of her nipples. He didn't stop until he got to her waist. His large hand smoothed over her hip and pulled her forward, trapping his steely erection between them.

Brea could feel the cool stainless ring resting against her abdomen. Her nipples tightened and wetness gathered between her thighs. She swore she'd climax without him even touching her if he didn't get a move on. Fire licked her veins, threatening to incinerate her.

His free hand threaded through her hair and tilted her head, giving her no choice but to meet his gaze. "Just so you know, that was fucking amazing."

"So why did you stop me?"

"Because when I come the first time with you—and I stress first time because it sure in the hell won't be the last—I want to be looking into your beautiful face, not staring down at the top of your head."

Brea didn't know why, but his confession brought moisture to her eyes. Damn her sentimental side. She blinked away the unwanted tears and worried her lower lip. Her fangs nicked the soft flesh, drawing vampire blood to the surface. She quickly ran her tongue over the tiny wound and sealed it. Even a drop of her blood could have detrimental consequences for Draven. She wasn't about to sentence him to a life of darkness, not when she planned to leave him in a few short hours.

"Then what the hell are you waiting on, barkeep?" Brea used her smart ass side to keep her emotions from getting tangled up. She couldn't allow her surfacing sentiments to stop her from taking flight when they were through. "I can feel myself getting older by the minute."

Draven growled, gripped her hips and easily lifted her from the floor. He seated her on his erection in one swift motion. Brea gasped. He filled her completely, and nothing had ever felt so right. She wrapped her legs around his trim waist.

"How's that for swift?" He raised one of his dark brows. "The question is... How hard do you want it?"

Brea gripped his long hair that he'd pulled up into a bun, and tightened her legs around his waist, digging her heels into his muscular ass. "You forget, barkeep. I'm a vampire. You might break the bed, but you aren't going to break me."

A chuckle rumbled out of him. "Something tells me I should be scared, but instead I just want to bang the shit out of you. So much for making love."

D RAVEN HAD WANTED TO EASE HER INTO IT, LOVE HER LIKE she deserved. Hell, she had been through so much already. Instead, her legs wrapped his waist with his erection buried to the hilt, while standing in the middle of a very crappy bedroom. Not a place he normally would think to lay his head, let alone fuck someone. His white, pristine apartment came to mind. This dusty old cabin was anything but clean. It could certainly use a hand from his cleaning lady.

We're not in Kansas anymore.

He wasn't sure why the old Wizard of Oz quote came to mind, but they were a long shot from home. Instead of *off to see the wizard*, they would soon be visiting someone more sadistic, someone with little regard for human life, someone responsible for thousands of deaths, either directly or indirectly. Draven hoped Brea succeeded in her desire to wipe Raúl's sorry ass from the planet. Draven would gladly aid her in her quest.

Her heels dug into his ass as she rocked on his erection, thankfully shutting out his troubling thoughts. The only thing that should matter at the moment was the sexy as hell woman arching beautifully before him, her small breasts but scant inches from his lips. He had never had a shortage of women, being the owner of a nightclub, but none of them compared to the woman now in his arms.

Brea tightened her grip on his hair. "Where the hell did you go, barkeep?"

Draven growled. "Wishing I wasn't about to toss you on a filthy mattress."

"There's a shower about fifteen feet behind us." Her smile widened, giving him a good view of her very white, very sharp fangs. "We can make use of that later."

With his palms cupping her smooth ass, he walked them to the nearest wall, using the wooden surface to drive himself deeper, not yet ready to make use of the bed.

Brea moaned.

Her breath hitched.

Nearly pulling out, Draven grit his teeth before slamming back into her, her walls tightening around him like a snug fist. Brea's back rode up the pine as Draven fucked her, giving Brea what she had asked for—hard. His blood pulsed through his ears. His balls tightened. The wooden paneling groaned beneath the pressure of his thrusts.

She leaned forward, licking the long column of his neck, her lips a hairbreadth from his carotid. Damn, if he didn't think about her sinking those razor-sharp fangs into him, almost wishing she would, adding to the already hot fucking sex. He was but a bite away from her blowing his mind.

Draven tried his damnedest to hold off his climax, knowing he was mere moments away. If she chose to sink her fangs, it would be all over. No two ways about it, she'd have a new term of endearment for him other than barkeep. Somehow, minute man didn't have quite the same effect.

He needed to stay focused, needed her all in if he were to catch her off guard. A shiver ran down his spine. Hell, the thought of taking her blood no longer disgusted him. He turned from the wall, grabbed her by the waist, and set her on her feet. Her gaze held questions, questions he'd answer in about … *oh, two-point-zero seconds.*

Tossing her to the bed, he gripped her ankles and pulled her forward so that her ass rested on the edge, her thighs spread. A small steel ring shimmered in the low light, piercing the back of her vulva.

"Oh, fuck … that is a beautiful thing."

A smile tipped her lips. "You like?"

"Are you kidding me right now? Fuuuuck."

Draven dropped to his knees and placed his hands on the inside of her thighs. He ran his nose up the soft flesh, catching the scent of her vanilla musk as he lightly caressed her skin with his fingers. Nipping the flesh, he used the pad of his tongue to soothe away the ache. A very long tongue that was about to make Brea a very conténted woman. He had heard the gossip around the club and some of his past lovers.

Brea gripped the hair at the top of his head and hissed.

"Greedy little thing, aren't you?"

"I swear if you don't allow me to come, barkeep, I'll make you regret the day we met."

He laughed. "I've trekked through the forest, been shot at, lived in this dump, and you don't think I might already regret it?"

She playfully slapped his arm, before her expression changed to one of concern. "Do you?"

"Hell no." He winked. "My only mission at the moment is making you cry out my name."

Her gaze flickered with humor. "Which one?"

"How many do you have for me?" he asked, leaving her chuckling. One hand stroking his cock, Draven used the other to slip a finger along her damp center. "Fuck, you're wet."

He leaned in, using his tongue to take the same path as his finger, earning him another moan. Her thigh muscles shivered and her head tilted into the mattress. He slid a finger into her while drawing her little bundle of nerves between his lips.

Brea squirmed. "Don't. Stop. Oh... God."

"That might just be my favorite nickname so far." Draven smiled, then licked another path up her folds.

"For once in your life, Draven. Shut. The. Hell. Up." She pulled his hair. "And do that again."

One of his brows rose with his amusement. "This you mean?"

He sucked her sensitive flesh between his teeth, toying with it using the tip of his tongue. Her walls trembled about his fingers, gripping them. Brea was damn close to climaxing. He could feel it in her response, see it in the swiftness of her breathing, and in the tightness in which she held him. Using both hands now, he spread her wide and replaced his fingers with his tongue. He circled the small ring in her vulva, traced a path up her center before dipping it inside.

Her thigh muscles tightened. Her limbs shook and she cried out, her orgasm washing over her. He glanced up, watching her. Damn, but that was a beautiful thing. Draven continued the assault until she pulled his head from between her thighs. He ran a palm down his whiskered jaw and looked down on a very sated Brea. Nothing had ever looked more beautiful.

His cock pained him, needing a release of its own. Draven shivered, not only because of Brea lying before him offering, but also over the concept of drinking her blood. From his understanding, he'd need very little. The thought scared the shit out of him.

Vampire.

And a mated one at that.

He hoped his mate would still be talking to him.

Brea smiled languidly, looking well-fucked. Draven was well past waiting. He stood, shucked his jeans and briefs, then knelt on the bed between her spread thighs. The mattress creaked and dipped beneath his added weight. He'd definitely want a repeat on his white satiny sheets when they made it home … *if* they made it home. Brea could have her pick of sides to his bed, though he'd much preferred her taking the spot beneath him.

She crooked a finger and he gladly obeyed, stopping just shy of touching her, taking her nakedness in. She was a gorgeous vision, one he'd never tire of looking at. Draven leaned down, cradled her face, and brushed his lips softly against hers, showing her what he wasn't ready to put into words. Binding her to him would not be a hardship, at least not from where he sat. As a matter of fact, he thought he might be getting the better end of the deal. He was doing it for her own safety, though she wouldn't see it that way. Brea might think of him as being saddled to another player.

After all, he had earned every bit of his reputation.

Only a coward would have agreed to her terms, promising her he'd stay behind. Like hell. Since she refused to allow him to follow her as a man, then he intended to do so as a blood-drinking vampire. Brea's argument would no longer hold water. If she failed in her crusade, then they'd go down together, a united front.

Draven deepened his kiss, possessing her, branding her to him. She was his and he wasn't about to share her, nor would he ever make her face disappointment in him. His erection slid along her folds, eliciting a groan. He couldn't hold out much longer.

"What are you waiting on, barkeep?"

Draven laughed. He had a feeling making love to her would never become stale. "I thought you needed recovery time. After all, I just gave you a brag-worthy climax."

Brea chuckled, rocking the just-fucked look. "Pretty sure of that tongue of yours, aren't you?"

"Confident. There's a difference." He flashed her his pearly whites. "I don't hear you complaining."

She gripped his hair and pulled him forward, their lips barely grazing. "And you won't either. Now, why not shut up and get busy giving me another climax worth bragging about?"

Draven growled. Taking her wrists in one of his hands, he pinned them over her head. He kissed a path down her neck, lightly nipping her soft flesh, before running his tongue along the same path, tasting the gathering salt. Bracing himself, he let go of her wrists and positioned his cock at her opening, sinking just the crown. His arms shook with the need to push forward.

"Gorgeous," he whispered, before fully sinking into her.

Her back arched, her breasts now just scant inches from his lips. Sucking one taut nipple between his lips earned him a moan. He suckled the tight bud, then circled it with his tongue, before giving the other one equal attention and tugging the tiny ring between his teeth. Kissing a path up her chest, he slanted his lips over hers, intertwining their fingers, pinning her hands overhead once again. Draven created a rhythm she easily followed, greedily raising her hips to meet him. Her walls gripped him, tighter than he had felt with any woman in his past. Jesus! Was that a vampire thing? If so, he damn well liked it.

Pure ecstasy.

Who needed the crap he used to peddle when drug-free you could reach the same fucking heights? He thought about biting her. She'd be damn pissed, maybe even refuse to ever fuck him again. If so, Draven needed this to count, just in case she decided to take his balls.

"Look at me, Brea."

Her dark gaze raised to his. She drew her bottom lip between her teeth. Brea was close to going over the edge. Increasing his rhythm, Draven released her wrists and reached between them to the spot they were joined. He circled her clit, adding pressure to the nerves.

"Don't hold back. Ah… *Fuck!*"

"Draven—" His name tumbled from her lips at the same time his orgasm squeezed out of him.

Her climax milked him as she tilted her head into the mattress, exposing her slender neck to him. Draven had seconds in which to act, to take complete advantage of Brea. He licked the slender column of her throat and bit … hard. The taste of her vampire blood filled his mouth, leaving him no room for regrets.

CHAPTER THIRTEEN

"W HAT THE HELL HAVE YOU DONE?" BREA WHISPERED as she watched Draven finally sleeping peacefully.

His actions had caused her to seriously delay her departure from the cabin, which was risky at best. Raúl no doubt had his men combing the area, and it had been nothing short of pure luck that kept them from being found.

Nearly a week had passed since Draven had so stupidly bit her out of some mixed up desire to protect her from her godfather. She hadn't needed his help. *Christ!* He had further complicated matters. What had she been thinking bringing him along? She should've known he would have stopped at nothing short of death to see her safe.

Since the first day she had walked into his nightclub, looking for Joseph, he had seemed to take it upon himself to be her knight in shining armor. His loyalty had mandated he follow his fallen friend's wishes. Trouble was, she didn't need saving. And she resented the fact he thought her so feeble he felt the need to turn himself into a bloodsucker … no matter how endearing his actions.

Then there was the sex.

It had been fantastic.

Thank goodness for Draven had sealed their fate when he took her blood, mating them. If by some miracle they walked away from this mess, the eternal binding couldn't be undone. Even though she tried to remain optimistic, Brea wasn't foolish enough to think they were above being taken out. Vampire or not, Joseph hadn't had a fighting chance. If Raúl decided he wanted someone dead, then there wasn't a whole lot they could do about it. He killed people without blinking, had done so for lesser sins.

Raúl wasn't about to be thrilled with the idea she'd taken on another mate. They weren't married, but Raúl wouldn't understand the difference. There was no such thing as divorce, no walking away once mated. Only death ended the alliance. Joseph had probably thought he could handle the monogamy when he had agreed to protect her from her godfather by mating with her. He had failed … in a big way.

She glanced back at Draven. Sweat beading his brow was the only lingering indication he had gone through a near week of hell. The fire burning beneath his flesh and through his veins wouldn't be something he'd ever forget. Joseph had held her through most of her change and absorbed some of the pain. She had tried to hold Draven, tried to soak up some of the agony. But it hadn't worked. Maybe because the male was supposed to take care of the female. What the hell did she know? Brea rolled her eyes.

Typical.

Even as vampires, the men were chauvinists.

Thank goodness the worst of it was over. Draven would need nourishment. As would she. Since his turning, his blood could no longer feed her. She could drink from him, pleasure in it even. But the substance she needed to stay alive could only be found in a human. Brea would need to take him into Tijuana where she could find a couple of humans to feed on, followed by hypnotizing them.

She glanced at her clasped hands as she sat cross-legged on the mattress next to Draven. The death chill had taken over her skin, making it nearly translucent. She was days past needing to feed, but she hadn't been able to bear leaving Draven's side.

What if Raúl's men happened upon him?

She might be weak due to the lack of blood, but Draven stood a better chance with her at his side. He needed the red cells to complete the change and gain his strength. Once he awoke, they'd be able to take the motorcycle into town and find a quiet little hole-in-the-wall bar. A quick trip for *fast food*. They'd be in and out, and back on the road with the humans completely unaware.

Draven stretched his long limbs. The sheet covering him slipped dangerously low on his hips, drawing her gaze down his chest, past his abs, to the happy trail heading for his groin. She licked her lips, desire shooting through her. This gorgeous man was *hers*.

Mated.

Brea thought about her mission, one that might see them both killed, and couldn't help but wonder if they weren't better off walking away. They'd be forced to live a life on the run, moving frequently, staying one step ahead of her godfather. She was sure there would be no getting Raúl to see reason.

She nibbled a fingernail, watching Draven's eyes move rapidly behind his eyelids, telling her he was in the throes of a dream. Running wouldn't be the answer. She wouldn't live her life in fear that her godfather might one day catch up to them. It was no way to live.

Brea needed to stop Raúl.

If not for her, then for Draven and his noble attempt to help her.

He groaned, a scowl on his lips. Exhaustion continued to claim him. Brea rested her back along the wall behind the bed and ran her fingers through her hair. Would Draven manage to remain faithful when his reasoning for mating had nothing to do with friendship, let alone love? Brea didn't think she could handle another infidelity.

Not with him.

She blinked, stopped by her thoughts.

Releasing a deep breath, she ran her palms down her face. The truth had sneaked up on her, taking her unaware. It might not have been love at first site, but Draven certainly had grown on her over the past few days. He made her laugh, frustrated her to no end, endeared her, and was an incredible lover. Leaving him behind was out of the question, which meant she had to take care of his needs.

Even before her own.

"Fuck!" Draven shifted on the mattress, attempting to sit. He groaned, before falling back to the mattress. "Please tell me the fire running through my veins isn't because I died and this is hell."

Brea smiled. There was the Draven she had fallen for, though now wouldn't exactly be the best time for confessions. "Welcome back to the living, barkeep."

"Please tell me it gets better."

"Once you feed."

He smacked his forehead with the heel of his hand. "Gross."

"Your fault." She scowled. "What the hell were you thinking anyway?"

"Ask me that when the hangover leaves."

"It isn't a hangover, Draven." Brea moved on the mattress so she sat on her knees beside him. "You are in serious need of … sustenance. You'll feel much better once you feed. Now get your sorry ass out of this bed so we can both get nourishment. I could have died here waiting on you."

"That's a bit extreme, don't you think?" The mention of taking care of her, though, got him moving, which had been her hope. Placing his feet on the wooden flooring, he stood, not bothering with the sheet. He stood gloriously naked, his backside to her. Brea resisted the urge to bite.

"Nice ass, vamp boy."

Draven shook his head as he stepped into his discarded pants. He pulled them over his lean hips and fastened them before turning around. Desire shot through her. Brea had a feeling she might have to get used to being in a constant state of arousal around him. He looked good enough to eat. As a matter of fact, the sex was about to get a whole lot better. So how did they top fantastic?

"I think I preferred barkeep."

"Not into being a sexy vampire?"

His nostrils flared. Draven placed his fists on his hips. "If you don't calm the fuck down, we will never get nourished."

Brea's gaze snapped up from the growing bulge in his pants to his darkening eyes. "I'm not sure what you mean?"

She lied. Brea knew exactly what he was referring to. His vampire senses were kicking in and he scented her desire. Brea drew her lower lip between her teeth. Her gaze traveled over the sparse hair on his chest and down to the waistband of his jeans. His bulge had definitely gotten bigger.

Draven growled. "You are one fucking cruel woman."

"How do you figure?" she asked, arching one of her brows.

"You know damn well I can smell you. Christ, if not for being so hungry, I'd be bending you over that filthy mattress and fucking you until you cried mercy. Instead, my gut wants to gnaw a hole right through the nasty thing."

She chuckled. Grabbing his shirt from the chair next to the bed, she tossed it to him. "Let's go get you something to eat. Then I'm going to hold you to that promise. Just so you know, barkeep, I'm a vampire. I won't cry mercy easily."

He smiled for the first time since awakening. "I'm counting on it, sweetheart."

CHAPTER FOURTEEN

D RAVEN PULLED THE MOTORCYCLE TO A STOP IN FRONT OF a small tavern on the outskirts of Tijuana. In hand-painted letters were the words *Casillero del Diablo*. Devil Locker … fitting since they were likely in the Devils' territory. The MC claimed California as their state, but he bet they easily slid into these parts of Mexico as well since they worked side-by-side with the La Paz cartel.

He kicked down the side stand and allowed Brea to step over the seat before he alighted. Taking off the black helmet, he placed it on the seat as he swept his gaze over the area. Very few milled about. A couple of stray dogs nosed for garbage in the adjacent alley, while a couple of kids played ball in the dirt streets. Draven would bet this place catered to the locals. It certainly didn't have a touristy vibe.

The rough-hewn siding could've used a good paint job. The peeling white paint left much of the dark wood beneath exposed. A neon sign flickered, advertising *Modelo*, in one of the two windows facing the street. Draven could appreciate a good Mexican beer.

Today was not going to be one of those days.

They were in search of something warm, thick, and disgusting. Not something they'd find on tap. Draven didn't want to think about his new form of nutrition, even if his stomach pained in hunger. The thought of the warm, crimson fluid nearly made him gag. He rubbed a palm down his whiskers, the scratch barely audible above the muted sound of the bass coming from the tavern.

The door opened and AC/DC's "Back in Black" spilled into the parking lot. A short, black-haired man exited the bar, his width damn near matching his height. Draven didn't miss the six-shooter holstered at his side as he lumbered by. Most men patronizing the joint likely carried firearms. He turned to Brea, who seemed completely at ease.

"You know anyone here?"

Brea smiled, her gaze turning up in humor. "They don't bite." She leaned in and whispered into his ear, "We do."

Skirting him, Brea walked over to the wooden door with a dirt smudged oval window and yanked it open, not bothering to see if he followed. *Christ!* He best get with the program or wind up dying of hunger. It already felt like he had a hole starting in his stomach about a mile wide. Brea was correct. They were the immortals, therefore they had the advantage.

Draven entered the tavern behind her. Other than Brea and the bartender, only one other man sat on a barstool, nursing a draft beer. He looked at the clock on the wall. It was still early, being only about half past eight. Draven knew all too well the bar life didn't get lively until after ten. He supposed if they got this over with quickly, they could be in and out... The door opened and two more men strode into the establishment, these two looking none too friendly. As a matter of fact, Draven would prefer to steer clear of them. He was about to suggest just that when Brea left him standing by the bar. She approached the two men, who had taken a booth at the far end of the bar next to another door with a red emergency exit sign hanging above it.

Okay, maybe allowing the little sprite to plan this whole feeding debacle wasn't the wisest of plans. She was going to get them a bullet right between the eyes. He allowed her a few moments before he walked up behind her and placed his hand possessively on the small of her back. Draven didn't want there to be any question as to whom she belonged to.

Brea turned, smiled warmly at him, then gave the gentleman her attention again. "So how about it?"

The larger of the two looked from Draven back to Brea. He pointed a light-brown finger in Draven's direction. "We don't have to fuck him, right?"

Brea chuckled, the sound deep, though not at all like her normal laugh. "Just me, big boy. That is if you think you can handle me. I take you two into the bathroom. You fuck me while I give him"—she pointed at the smaller of the two, which wasn't saying much because he was still fairly good in size—"a blow job."

"What's he gonna do?" the smaller of the two asked. He patted the sheathed hunting knife at his side. "If the fucker thinks to rob us, we'll gut you both."

Brea leaned down and braced her hands on the table, probably giving them a pretty good shot of the brassiere she wore beneath her sweater. "He's going to watch. We're kinky that way."

"Fuck that." The bigger one shook his head. "I don't know what kind of shit you're into, but you can forget it. I'd just as soon put a bullet in his head than have him watch while I fuck you."

Draven was seconds from fisting her sweater and dragging her ass out of there. Quite frankly, her tactics sucked.

"Whoa, Joe. I'm all about that little *señorita* wrapping her lips around my cock. I don't give a fuck if the *fresa* watches or not.

This was about to take a turn for the ugly. Before he could stop Brea, she headed for the door marked *Señoritas*. The smaller man slid from the booth and quickly followed, leaving Joe cursing up a blue streak before standing and following his buddy through the door. Draven sighed. Nope, this was not going to end well. By the time he reached the door, not a sound could be heard on the other slide, not even with his enhanced hearing from his newly acquired vampire genetics. Draven eased the door open to find both men, standing side-by-side with a dazed look on their faces.

Fuck! He had missed all the fun.

"You so have to show me how to do that." Draven shook his head. He had a lot to learn. "That was quick."

"It doesn't take long to hypnotize someone, barkeep. Just get them to look you into the eyes and say the right words."

Brea grabbed Joe's arm and held it out to Draven. His damn fangs had a mind of their own, no matter what his thoughts had to say about it, and punched through his gums.

The tips scraped his bottom lip, attesting to their razor-sharpness. Brea had already fully transformed, gorgeous in her vampire self. He couldn't wait to get her back to the cabin. His eyes heated as they transformed into the endless black pools, mirroring Brea's.

Without thought, Draven brought the forearm to his nose and sniffed, the rich, heady scent pleasing to his palate. He easily sank his fangs into the man's wrist. Joe's succulent blood smoothed over his tongue and down his throat, quickly soothing the ache in his stomach. Draven had to fight the urge to gag. It certainly wouldn't look good in front of Brea if he wound up on his knees, dry-heaving. He supposed the flavor would one day grow on him. Heat blossomed, starting in his stomach and branching out, spreading from the tips of his toes to the top of his skull. He continued to drink, to suck the man's wrist when Brea's hand touched his forearm.

"Lick the wounds closed, Draven."

He released his fangs, wiping the back of his hands across his wet lips and staining his flesh red. "But I'm still ravenous."

"You'll learn to control it." When he didn't do as she instructed, Brea leaned down and did it for him. "You only take what you need. We don't hurt those who mean us no harm."

With these two, Draven could seriously debate that issue with her. "Fine. But just so you know, you're responsible if I'm hungry again in twenty minutes."

She chuckled and patted his abs. "You'll survive, big guy."

"So what do we do with these two?"

"After I take my fill, we leave."

"What happens to them?" Draven nodded toward the two men.

Brea shrugged. "They'll snap out of it in about ten minutes and wonder why the hell they are in the ladies' room by themselves. By then, we'll be long gone."

CHAPTER FIFTEEN

BREA WALKED AROUND THE CABIN, FRESH FROM THE shower, sporting a pair of light blue skinny jeans and a silky pink tank she had acquired while they were in Tijuana. They had taken a quick detour from the tavern to a twenty-four hour Walmart to purchase a few changes of clothes. The last ones had to be pretty ripe smelling as hand washing only went so far.

From where he sat on the sofa, he definitely liked the new outfit. The tips of his fangs were already punching through his gums. Draven barely had a leash on his vampire side. Brea had wanted to get on the road and all Draven wanted to do was toss her back on that bed, filthy mattress be damned.

"I can smell you, you know," Brea said as she tossed clothes into a new backpack.

She was preparing to hit the road, had said as much on their way back to the cabin. No time for dallying.

"I showered."

"Not that, barkeep." She shook her head and laughed. He definitely liked the sound of it. "Your desire."

He shrugged, not feeling the least apologetic. "Can I help it? Christ! I want to jump you. How about we fuck, then hit the road."

Brea turned and placed her hands on her hips. Her warm smile smoothed over him like a lover's caress, not helping his situation. "As good as that sounds, we already spent way too much time in one location. It's only a matter of time before my godfather's men stumble over this cabin. We've already pushed our luck. We needed to be on our way to Ensenada days ago. Your little plan derailed us. Of which, by the way, we still haven't discussed. Mating is not done without the president of the Sons of Sangue's consent. You know this."

Draven stood and closed the distance between them. He placed his hands on her shoulders, looking down on her. His black vampire gaze reflected back at him in her brown gaze. Her words were doing nothing to cool down said desire. Razor-sharp fangs teased his lips. *Damn!* Hard-ons were hard enough to conceal. How did one conceal fangs?

"Fuck, Hawk," he said, meaning it. "First of all, the pissy club P doesn't even know about you, thanks to you and Kinky breaking those rules already. Second, I'm not a member of his precious MC, so he can't order me around."

"What do you intend to do then, Draven? About me ... *us* when we get back to the states. *If* we make it back."

Draven framed her face in his palms, leaned down, and slanted his lips over hers. Just a gentle meeting of lips. One to show her how he cherished her. He hoped one day she'd come around and care for him, love him even.

"We *will* get back, sweetheart. I won't allow anything happen to you. Not while I draw breath."

One of her dark brows arched. "What's your reasoning for taking my blood without my permission, Draven? To protect me?"

"You're pissed."

"Yes." She hung her head before he tipped it back up using his crooked forefinger, forcing her to look at him. "Okay, maybe not pissed. More like annoyed. I understand your motives, but what you did wasn't right. You should've asked for my permission."

"You wouldn't have given it."

She stood silent for a long moment. Finally, she admitted, "No, I wouldn't have. But it would have been for your own good."

"I get to decide what's good for me."

"Like you decided for me? Had you for once considered I might not have wanted to mate with you? For crying out loud, Draven, it's for all eternity. It's not something you decide upon lightly, or because you want to protect someone."

Her comment stung, a low blow, though he supposed it was nothing less than he deserved. Brea's gaze darted away, but not before he detected the moisture there. It cut him straight to the heart. No, he hadn't considered her feelings. His actions might have been noble, but never had he thought about what would happen once they put Ensenada behind them.

Draven took a deep breath. He had been a damn selfish bastard.

"I'm sorry, Brea." And he was. When this was over, he'd find a way to fix it. "I only meant to help, not saddle you with an unwanted mate. You deserve better after Kinky—"

"Leave Kinky out of this." Her gaze snapped back, the sorrow replaced with anger. "*He* didn't deserve me."

"You're right." He ran the pad of his thumb over her lower lip. "And you deserve better than me. I took advantage of you. Now, because of my selfish desire, you're stuck with me."

"That's where you're wrong, Draven." Her gaze shifted black and her voice grew thick with her fangs. "*I* don't deserve you. You took me in when you didn't have to. You followed me to Mexico on a witch hunt. You were shot at. And now … now, you've become the thing you despise. All out of some mixed-up notion that I need saving."

"Brea…"

"Let me finish, barkeep. I may be a vampire, which makes me physically stronger. But inside … emotionally? I'm a wreck. My scars you can't see. My godfather? He wants to fuck me. How messed up is that? It's not that I don't want you in my world, Draven." Brea reached up and ran a palm down his whiskered cheek. "I don't want to screw up your world by having me in it."

Was she for real? Before her, he'd fucked his way through endless women. Most of them, he couldn't remember their names, let alone their faces once dawn hit. He couldn't get in and out of their beds fast enough, and rarely had he slept with one more than once. With Brea? He couldn't wait to get her into his bed again. *Christ!* He never wanted her out of it. This woman had turned his world upside down.

They may not have met under the best of circumstances, but he was damn sure glad they did. He'd never regret the day she walked into his bar, looking for Joseph. Not that he would've ever wished the biker dead. But because he met an untimely death, Draven had been the one to profit. And damn him, he couldn't say he regretted it. He never would, regardless how damaged she thought herself to be.

Draven scented her desire, just as she had his earlier. Knowing he was the cause of that desire hardened his cock and stiffened his resolve to take her … now. Fuck the cartel. They had lasted this long without being found, they could damn well wait another hour. Draven wasn't about to be denied.

Backing Brea to the wall behind her, he reached for the hem of her tank and yanked it over her head. Her breath caught, but she didn't stop him. Instead, she reached for the button on his jeans, slid it from the hole and pulled down his zipper. She slipped her hand inside and wrapped her long fingers around him. Draven hissed. His balls tightened.

He leaned his forehead against hers, deftly flicking the front closure of her bra with his fingers and exposing her perky breasts. His mouth salivated. He had to taste one. Hell, his fangs ached to taste her. Lowering his head, he wrapped his lips around one nipple, toying with the tight bud with his tongue. Not able to control the urge, he sank his fangs into the soft flesh of her breasts. Brea groan, her grip on his erection tightened.

"Please, Draven." She gasped. "Oh my…"

Her words died out as he sucked her flesh, taking his fill before he licked close the twin holes. "I need to fuck you, sweetheart. We aren't leaving until that happens."

"God… *Please*."

Draven disentangled her grip, picked her up, and headed for the lone bedroom. He smiled down at her. "This won't take long."

Brea laughed. "That excited to be inside of me, barkeep?"

He winked at her. "You have no idea."

CHAPTER SIXTEEN

"DRAVEN!" BREA SHOVED HIS SHOULDER.

Sometime after their third bout of lovemaking, they'd both fallen into an exhausted sleep. So much for getting on the road. God forbid if they dallied overlong. He rolled over and threw his arm around her waist, cocooning her into his embrace. Instead of staying where she desired, Brea slipped from his arms and slid off the bed.

"Come back to bed, sweetheart."

He turned to his back and stretched. The sheet to dipped, barely covering his groin. Lord, he was magnificent. Even having recently loved every inch of him, her hunger to have him again continued to blossom.

Brea paused, turning her head as she heard the slight rustle of foliage. *Shit!* "We need to go … now!"

Draven sat, likely hearing the same stirring of brush. He stood and quickly moved to the bedroom's lone window. Using his finger to nudge aside the curtain, he briefly peered out. The cloth fluttered back into place. Grabbing his discarded jeans, he stepped into them before jogging from the room. Brea wasted no time pulling on her pants and tank, following him. Thank goodness she'd had the aforethought and packed their backpack the night before. It sat on the table, along with the keys to the motorbike. Draven made his way to each window and carefully took in their outside surroundings, assessing the situation.

Finished, he turned to her and whispered, "Three men. My best guess is left side of the cabin is unguarded since there is only a tiny window. One large enough for you to slip through."

"What do we do?"

"You take the backpack. Head for the bike. The helmets are on the seat."

"What about you?"

"Once I hear the bike's engine, I'll meet you where it's stashed." He gripped her forearms and pulled her to him, kissing her soundly. "It's showtime, sweetheart. Once you get to the bike, you count to five then start the engine. If I'm not there, you head the fuck out of here."

"No—"

He tipped her chin. "No arguments. Count to five and go."

Draven released her and turned her toward the table with the backpack. The sound of wood scraping against the aging frame sounded loud to her ears. She prayed it would go undetected by the men creeping up on the cabin. Brea returned to Draven's side and allowed him to hoist her up. Tossing the backpack to the ground, she slipped silently through. Once her feet touched the ground, Brea did a quick sweep of the area and waited to hear fast approaching feet. Only the sounds of the forest thankfully greeted her. A quick glance back at the window, she caught a glimpse of Draven in his glorious vampire form.

Her heart swelled.

Don't you die, vampire. I need you.

And if she ever got them out of this mess, she planned on telling him just how much.

Picking up the pack, she quickly stole through the dense foliage, ducking beneath low hanging branches and stepping over fallen debris. A couple hundred feet from the cabin, she came across the bike hidden from view of the dirt road. Thank goodness her godfather's men had somehow missed it. She slipped her leg over the seat, shrugged on the backpack, and kicked up the stand. Pulling on the helmet, she tightened the strap beneath her chin.

Her heart raced. Brea couldn't stand the idea of allowing Draven to contend with Raúl's men on his own. She should've never agreed to his cockamamie plan. If she hit five and he wasn't there, fuck his plan. She was going back to get him. If they harmed one hair on his gorgeous head, she'd personally bleed every one of those fuckers out.

Brea put the key into the ignition.

"One."

A man's scream had Brea's breath catching in her chest.

"Two."

The strong scent of human blood elongated her fangs.

"Three."

Rustling of brush came from her right. Another scream was cut short.

"Four."

The smell of blood was thick in the air. A third shout stopped her count when Draven rushed through the thick foliage, his white tee stained red. He jumped on the back of the bike and strapped on his helmet.

"Go," he shouted over the sound of the engine.

Brea picked up her feet, hit the gas, and they sped down the dirt road. Now wasn't the time to ask questions. Nor was she about to stick around to see if more of Raúl's men lurked by. Pulling back on the rubber handle grip, the bike sped off down the dirt road.

BREA PULLED THE MOTORCYCLE INTO a parking lot of a rest stop along 1D. The last road sign indicated they were about ten miles outside of Ensenada. Following their mad dash, Brea and Draven had ridden in silence. The stench of blood clung to Draven's shirt. She needed to get him out of his clothes and washed up before someone spotted them. The last thing they needed was to wind up in a Mexican jail.

Opening the backpack, she pulled out a new tee and pair of jeans and tossed them at him. He caught the clothes, remaining annoyingly quiet. Brea was dying for the details. What he had done had to be weighing heavy on his mind. He'd need to talk about it. Setting the helmet on the bike, Draven barely spared her a glance before heading for the men's room at the end of the long sidewalk. Minutes later, he emerged carrying a plastic sack containing his soiled clothes. He stuffed them into the side satchel of the motorcycle. Later, they'd need to ditch them.

"What happened back there?" she finally asked, no longer able to take his silence.

His face hardened. "What needed to be done."

Draven no doubt thought of himself as a cold-blooded murderer, even if it had been done in self-defense. Her heart ached for him. He'd not likely think it made much of a difference. And truthfully? She couldn't imagine what was going through Draven's mind since she had yet to take a human life herself.

"Want to talk about it?"

"Not particularly."

He grabbed his helmet, but she placed her hand on it and prevented him from placing it back on his head, shutting her out. "Talk to me."

"What the fuck do you want me to say, Brea?" he all but growled. "That those three men back there won't be hurting anyone again? Because they won't. By the time I finished, it looked like a brown grizzly, or some other wild animal, tore out their throats."

He looked to the pavement with a slow shake of his head. Her chest seized all the more. Brea prayed the fun-loving man she had first met still existed somewhere within him. She'd hate to be the reason his nature had been forever altered.

"I'm sorry." Tears welled in her eyes, moments away from becoming a blubbering mess. This was certainly not the time for her to lose her shit. "I'm so damn sorry."

Draven stepped around the bike separating them and framed her face, running the pads of his thumb beneath her eyes. "Don't waste your tears, sweetheart. Not for me. I did what needed to be done to protect you. I will continue to do the same until I draw my last breath. Understand? We'll find a way out of this."

Brea worried her lower lip as she sucked back the tears. "You deserve better."

"I deserve you, sweetheart. You say that one more fucking time and I swear I'll throw you over my knee and spank that sweet ass of yours. Right before I fuck you. Now how about we get the hell out of here. Once we find Raúl, we can do what needs done and head back home."

He tipped her chin, then slanted his lips over hers, slipping his tongue into her warmth. She tangled her fingers in his hair, returning his kiss, showing him what her words had not yet expressed.

When he stepped back, his gaze held hers. "*Our* home."

CHAPTER SEVENTEEN

R AÚL TREVINO CABALLERO SAT AT THE END OF HIS TEN AND a half foot dining table. Ten ladder-back chairs flanked the long sides while two, gray cloth-covered chairs decked each end. The sun colored the horizon red, making for a stunning ocean view as he peered out the large picture window. He sat alone, drinking from a 1951 bottle of Dalmore Selene whisky. He loved the combined tastes of coffee, chocolate, marmalade, and cinnamon and only opened the bottle on special occasions.

Today was once such occasion.

The last he'd heard, his men had found Brea … *his* Brea. The bar owner traveling with her was a mere inconvenience. Just as the biker she considered herself married to had been. He had been easy pickings. Raúl's marksman had aimed for the T-box on his face and planted the bullet right between the fucker's eyes. The man dropped like a rag doll, not standing a chance.

Pulling a Cuban cigar from the wooden box before him, he ran the stogie beneath his nose. It smelled much like the rain-soaked earth—rich soil. Raúl picked up his personalized cigar cutter, a present from Fidel Castro, as were the cigars, and cut off the tip. The two had been introduced about a decade ago and had been friends ever since. Picking up his butane lighter, he toasted the end of the cigar until it began to smolder. Raúl placed the large stogie between his lips and took short puffs until the cigar tip glowed red.

Smoke rings left his lips, floating toward the ceiling, while he envisioned the moment Brea Gotti stepped over his threshold. If she refused to stay as his guest, Raúl wasn't above keeping her prisoner. Eventually, she would come to realize, due to family obligations, that she belonged with him. Raúl was not a man to be denied. He had allowed her insubordination for far too long. Her lithe body would be a welcomed addition to his king-size bed.

His dick hardened at the thought.

Christ! She looked as if she had a tight little pussy.

Raúl would take great pleasure in breaking her in. He'd gladly take and possess every hole of hers and wipe away the memory of the dirtbag she lived with, not to mention the bar owner if she had made the mistake of fucking him as well.

No matter. He looked across the darkening horizon. By now, the Blood 'n' Rave would be orphaned and looking for new ownership. A smile crossed his lips. Raúl was used to getting his way.

Correction. He always got his way.

It was time Brea Gotti realized that. After all, knowing the big heart his godchild had, she wouldn't want to be responsible for any more young men's deaths. Didn't she realize he could give her the world? He took great pleasure in knowing he was among some of the richest men in the world. He could and would buy his wife anything she asked for, anything her heart desired.

A quick glance at the clock had him wondering what was taking his men so long. By now they should've checked in, apprised him of the situation. The last time he had talked to Jon, they were only a few hundred yards from the old cabin. Jon had personally sneaked up on the shack and spotted Brea and the bar owner in residence. He had retreated to call Raúl and to retrieve his orders. They were simple. Kill the bar owner, and take Brea unharmed, but by any means necessary. To come home without her meant they signed their own death certificates. Raúl wasn't a forgiving man. He was a man of action.

His gaze dropped to the burner phone lying beside the cigar box. He hated the weakness sluicing through his veins, for surely with uncertainty came shortcomings. Raúl needed to get Brea beneath his rule. He couldn't allow the lapse in his control a moment longer. Picking up the cell, he punched the number to Jon's phone. Several rings later, the call went to voice mail.

"Son of a bitch." Raúl tossed the phone to the table, the clunk echoing about the vast empty room. He was quickly losing his patience.

Louis, his close second in command walked into the room, obviously hearing the racket and coming to check on him out of concern. One of his dark, bushy brows rose. "You okay?"

"Have you heard from Jon?"

The man ran a hand through his loose curls, pushing the black hair from his face. At six-foot-six, two-hundred-sixty pounds of muscle, very few men were brave enough to piss with him. That's why Raúl liked having him at his side. That and there weren't many who were as loyal.

"Not a word. You worried?"

"Last I heard they had found her. What the fuck is taking them so long? I swear if they come back empty-handed, I'll personally cut their hearts out. How fucking hard is it to take a five-foot-two, one-hundred-pound little slip of a girl?"

Louis remained silent. Not that Raúl expected an answer from him. "How many men are here?"

"Three." Louis rested his hand on the M16 draped over his shoulder. "We left the rest back in La Paz. Since we hadn't heard from Jon and his men, I sent three more to check on them."

Raúl chuckled. "For a fucking bar owner? How hard can it be to kill the son of a bitch? I swear I'll cut their balls off if they're fucking around."

"That leaves the three here for your protection, including me."

It was Raúl's turn to raise a brow "You think that was wise?"

"It's been a quiet night. I think we're good."

"You stay here in the dining room with me." He reached into his cigar box and tossed Louis one. "Share a drink with me."

Raúl grabbed a clean glass from the buffet behind him and slid it down the table. Louis grabbed his cell from his holster on his side, punched his finger onto the gorilla glass a few times, then placed it to his ear. A few moments later, he set his cell on the table, took a seat a few down from Raúl, and helped himself to the whisky.

"They took the Hummer. They should be to the cabin in less than a half hour."

"Good."

"You all right?"

Raúl narrowed his gaze. "Why the fuck do you ask?"

"Because normally nothing fazes you." He took a sip of the whisky, then smiled in appreciation. "That's smooth."

"At twelve-thousand a bottle, it best be."

"So what has you bugged?"

Raúl took a pull from his cigar and blew smoke rings again, watching as they dissipated. "Normally, I'd say you're correct. But something about this doesn't sit right with me. Jon should've checked in long ago."

"We'll find them. Maybe they just dropped their cell."

He supposed that was a simple enough explanation. Brea could be a real hellcat. He had seen it in her as a child. "They get back here, they best hope that's what the fuck happened. Failure is not an option."

"I think you're letting her get the best of you, boss."

Raúl's gaze heated. How dare Louis question him? "You watch your mouth, boy."

He held up one of his hands in front of him. "No disrespect meant. I only meant that your men have your best interests at heart. I'm betting they will be walking through that door with her in tow in no time."

"You better be right." He reached down and adjusted the crotch to his fitted dress pants. "I plan to be fucking her by midnight."

Louis smiled as he took a puff from his own Cuban. "You'll probably be fucking like rabbits all night."

"You can count on that." Raúl laughed robustly. "It will be your job to keep the men from my wing of the house. I'm going to take my time fucking that pussy."

"Excuse me." Antonio stepped around the corner. "You have company, Raúl."

"Who the fuck—"

"Well hello to you too, Raúl."

Spike, the new president of the Devils MC, strode into the room as if he owned the place, followed by a few choice words from Raúl. He was the last fucking person he had expected to see.

"To what do I owe the pleasure, Spike?" Raúl grumbled.

"I need a huge fucking favor."

Raúl puffed on his Cuban, eyeing the scrawny biker. He was a scrappy little fucker with a set of huge *cajones*. "Exactly why would I want to grant you one?"

"You hated Tank. I took care of that for you."

"How so? My sources told me that big biker from the Sons of Sangue took him out. I believe his name was Rogue."

"Had it not been me convincing the DEA that I was Tank, he'd still be alive and in jail, singing like a canary. Me? I'm all about working with you." The biker tossed a duffle to the table. "Money Tank skimmed from your profits. You're welcome."

Raúl nodded to Louis, who grabbed the bag and unzipped it. A grin split his face at the large stacks of US dollars filling the bag, earning Spike his favor.

"So why are you standing here and not behind bars?"

"Because the feds didn't have shit on me. All their evidence pointed to Tank and he's ash. When they realized they had the wrong guy, I walked."

Raúl indicated the man should sit. Once he followed the directive, Raúl said, "It appears I might be in a giving mood. What is it you need?"

He leaned back in the chair and crossed his arms behind his grimy blond head. "You hate the Sons of Sangue."

"I do."

"They have something that belongs to me. I want it back."

"You have an MC of your own. Why not take the Devils and go get it?"

"I lost quite a few men to the DEA, not to mention the ones Rogue took out. And since I'm a few men short, I thought you might lend me a hand."

His gaze traveled to the bag of money. There had to be at least a half a million in there. Spike could have run off with it. Instead, he chose to bring it back. Whatever the Sons of

Sangue had, must be worth a lot to Spike to return that kind of cash.

"You have my word that we'll help you get back what it is they have of yours." Raúl paused, carefully eyeing Spike. "You fuck with me, and I'll see you as dead as Tank."

The burner phone on the table rang, taking his attention from the biker. Raúl snatched it up. "Talk to me."

His man on the other end cleared his throat. "Sorry, boss. You have three dead men out here. Looks like their fucking throats were ripped clean off. The girl and the bar owner are nowhere to be found."

Raúl didn't wait to hear any more. He whipped the phone against the plastered wall, where it shattered into tiny pieces. Standing, the chair he had been sitting on tipped and fell to the floor with a thud.

He quickly dismissed the biker and addressed Louis. "Get him a room upstairs, make sure he stays put, and lock this fucking place down. No one gets in and no one leaves. Got it?"

Louis gripped Spike by the biceps, pulling him from the chair. "You can't fucking keep me here like a prisoner." Spittle flew from his mouth.

Raúl narrowed his gaze. "I can do as I please. Get the fuck out of my sight. We'll talk again later. You want to live, then do the fuck as I say."

Raúl stood alone, watching his men do his bidding. Louis and Antonio stayed on the main floor with him, while Francisco took Spike upstairs and secured him in one of the spare rooms. Francisco would make sure the biker stayed put or he'd answer to Raúl. He was no fool. Raúl knew damn well what he was dealing with when it came to his spirited god-daughter. She might be a vampire, but he had a surprise of his own. Rocking back on his heels, his white fangs mirrored back at him in the reflection of the window.

CHAPTER EIGHTEEN

DRAVEN STOPPED THE BIKE AND KILLED THE ENGINE, PARK-ing in a barren lot down the coast from Raúl's mon-strosity he called a beach-front vacation home. It was easily the largest dwelling on this stretch of the beach. Night had fallen hours ago. The large full moon cast a beam across the ocean, lighting up the evening sky and not giving them much for cover. Raúl's men would easily spot them coming from a half mile away. He hoped luck would be on their side and the men he'd taken out at the cabin would leave few here at the coastal home. If they were to accomplish Brea's goal of get-ting inside and confronting her godfather one-on-one, then they'd need to catch Raúl and his team off guard.

Small waves rolled up along the shore, scenting the air with salt water. Seagulls took flight as he and Brea left the bike behind and headed down the sandy beach. A quick glance at her, told Draven the bravado she wore like a badge was beginning to slip the closer they came to Raúl's. She pursed her lips and blew out a steady stream.

"You going to be okay?" Draven asked, ready to abort the mission if that was indeed her wish.

She gave him a quick nod, her gaze trained straight ahead. "He needs to be stopped."

"He's your godfather, Brea." Draven paused and gripped her biceps, gaining her attention.

Tears swam in her beautiful dark eyes. "He is, but that does not excuse him from being a bad person."

"Maybe not." He ran a knuckle down her cheek. "That doesn't make him any less a part of your past either. Your memories of him couldn't have all been bad."

"They weren't. When I was little, they shielded me from the truth. As I got older, that's when I realized my youth was nothing but lies, what my father and Raúl wanted me to be-lieve, what every child wants the men in their life to be. They were far from heroes. That's why I never again contacted my godfather after my father died."

"And Raúl thought you would one day return to him?"

"He did." She hung her head, toying with the sand be-neath her feet. "I never gave him the impression I would. When I learned what kind of a person he was, the murders he was presumably responsible for, I began to hate the man behind the facade."

Brea glanced back up, her gaze hardened. "The man I knew as a child is dead to me. I had hoped I could leave be-hind my past, never see him or his men again. I was wrong."

"What exactly do you hope to accomplish, sweetheart?" He needed to know before they stormed Raúl's home if Brea wanted the man dead or alive. He didn't need her regrets when all was said and done. "Tell me what the plan is."

She sucked in a shaky breath. "I want to talk to him, Dra-ven. If there is no reasoning with him, then I will take him out myself. Any of his men standing in our way, don't underestimate them. If they work for my godfather, they are cold-blooded killers. Drain them. If you hesitate, they will kill you."

He nodded. It went without saying, he would do what he needed to do to keep her alive, just as he had back at the cabin. Draven had never before taken a life, and yet when faced with the need to eliminate the men, he had done so without hesitation.

He would do so again.

Brea started down the stretch of beach and Draven fell into step beside her, taking one long stride to her two. They traveled the rest of the way in companionable silence. This time of night, they were completely alone on the beach. A few of the homes lining the ocean front still had lights on, spilling into the night.

Before long, they stopped about a football field away from her godfather's. Wrought iron gates lined the perimeter, rising into the night like the gates to Hades. Terraces on the top floor were no doubt strategically placed so his men would have great views from all sides. They'd need to be careful from here on out. It would be hard to spot a man aiming a rifle at their foreheads. He would bet they had *shoot first, ask questions later* orders.

"We go in together?"

Brea looked at him. "Maybe we should split up. You go along the side to the front, and I'll go through the back. Even though you're still new to this whole vampire thing, your strength should be stronger than theirs. Any locked door would be easy enough for you to twist the knob and shatter the cylinder. Try to be quiet about it. I have no idea how many of his men are inside."

He smiled at her. "There are at least three less."

"There are." She took a step forward, grabbed his nape, and pulled him down for a deep kiss. Had the situation not been so dire, he might have thought about a little sex on the beach. Brea released him just as quickly. "I'll see you inside."

As she meant to jog off, Draven called out. She turned and their twin black gazes met. "Don't get yourself killed."

"And if I do?"

"Not an option. Not in my plans for you."

The white tips of her fangs shown just below her upper lip. "Looking forward to it, barkeep."

Draven watched her for a moment while her lithe body easily ate up the sand. To anyone looking, they might think she was out for a late night jog. Finally glancing away and getting his head into the game, his gaze rose to the two terraces facing the ocean. They appeared empty. Had anyone been up there watching, they'd no doubt be leaning into view, trying to get a better view of the pretty young thing running along the shore. What men Raúl did have in residence probably watched the front of the property.

Satisfied, Draven slipped between two beach homes and around to the front drive. He stayed close the houses, ducking beneath windows, hoping to stay out of sight from Raúl's terraces. Draven paused, listening for any kind of movement. His keen hearing picked up the soft thud of Brea's feet hitting cement, at least it was his hope. He doubted any of Raúl's men were light enough to land as softly.

So good so far.

Draven easily leaped the wrought iron fencing, landing on the grass next to the brick paved sidewalk. He slipped around to the ten-foot-tall arched double doors, made of black wrought iron and glass. A light within the house glowed softly, but Draven couldn't see anyone moving about from his position. He tried the lever style handset to the door, only to find the dead bolt securely in place. He shook his head. Now fucking what? There was no knob to turn to break any kind of cylinder as Brea had suggested. His only option would be to break the glass and turn the dead bolt, which would alert the entire fucking household.

Plan B. He quickly jogged down the steps and around the side of the estate, hoping to find Brea, praying he wasn't too late.

Unfortunately, luck wasn't always on his side.

CHAPTER NINETEEN

THE HAIR RAISED ON BREA'S NAPE. A SENSE OF UNEASE washed over her. She tiptoed across the concrete patio to the French doors opening into the kitchen. Skirting the oversized patio furniture, she kept to the railing and out of view of the back doors. The layout was an open concept, leaving her very little cover once she entered the premises. Her godfather liked to sit at the dining room table with a cup of coffee or a whisky, depending on the time of day, all while smoking his expensive Cuban cigars. Even now the scent wafted to her nose, telling her he was indeed in residence. The strong pungent smell masked most orders. Even with her enhanced scent, she couldn't detect if he was alone.

Testing the door, she found it unlocked. Something was amiss. Her godfather never left a door unsecured, especially at this time of night. Raúl hadn't gotten this far by being a careless man. The fact the door was unlocked told her he expected company.

Shit!

She needed to get to Draven, warn him before he went in ready to kick ass, when it might be very well his own ass getting handed to him. The house might not appear alive with activity but Brea knew Raúl lay in wait. All of her instincts told her that her godfather was well aware of her presence.

121

Draven's scent wafted to her nose just before he leaped over the railing, landing softly beside her. Her heart raced. Brea was not about to put him in the line of fire again.

"We need to get out of here, Draven," she whispered.

Before he could respond, one of the French doors swung inward. Raúl stood on the other side, a large smile pasted on his thick lips. His scent hit her full on.

Mother of God!

"Going somewhere?" White fangs hung just below her godfather's upper lip. "Please … come in."

His polite request was nothing more than a thinly veiled demand, backed up by the two other presences she felt arrive behind her and Draven. No doubt assault rifles were trained on their backs. Steeling her resolve, Brea entered her godfather's kitchen, followed by Draven, who remained blessedly silent. His sarcasm would not be well received here. She prayed he allowed her to do the talking.

"Sit, please." Raúl's beefy hand indicated the ladder-back chairs flanking his cloth covered one he righted, making her wonder what had gone on before to find the chair upended.

The two men at their backs followed them into the house, stopping at the entrance to the dining room. While far enough to give them privacy, they were close enough to hear the exchange and take Brea and Draven out if Raúl decided he was no longer in the mood to entertain. And by out, she didn't mean leave the premises. She wasn't foolish enough to believe Raúl would keep her from harm if he deemed her no longer worthy. While she took one of the chairs and sat next to Raúl, Draven remained standing, bracing his hands on the polished wood surface.

"Why the fuck do you even want her, man?" Draven asked. Stirring the hornet's nest was a bad idea, so was questioning her godfather. "She's like half your age. Don't you think that's kind of gross from where she comes from, grandpa?"

Dear, Lord, help her. He was going to get them both shot.

Raúl's face reddened. A muscle ticked in his cheek. Brea figured up to this point, her godfather was simply humoring the barkeep. Draven should've considered himself lucky he wasn't shot on sight. She hoped her *if looks could kill* gaze kept his mouth shut from saying anything further.

Raúl snarled, his razor-sharp fangs filling his mouth. Brea cursed beneath her breath for not having detected the scent of another vampire before he stood before her. The strong aroma of his Cubans had masked his scent well. She was sure he had smoked one for that very purpose, knowing she might attempt to sneak in under the cover of night.

"You're living on borrowed time, *pendejo*." He pointed a beefy finger at Draven. "I should have you executed now. Are you responsible for taking out three of my good men? Or would that be my little *chiquita*?"

Brea hoped to get Raúl off the subject of Draven killing his men. If he suspected Draven was the one behind their throats being ripped out, he'd have Draven killed without question.

"How long?" she asked.

Raúl redirected his attention. One of his thick black brows rose. "For what, *chiquita*?"

"How long have you been hiding the fact you were a vampire?"

He chuckled. "Long before you were made one by that dirtbag you called a mate."

Brea was dumbfounded. How the hell had this escaped the Sons of Sangue? "Who turned you?"

"When Kane's son, Ion, was being held prisoner by my brother and me for his mother's crimes against us. His mother, Rosalee … pretty woman"—he paused as though envisioning the crazy bitch—"thought she could outsmart us. She found out otherwise. Ion was good enough to give me some of his blood before I staked him."

"Surely not of his own accord."

"It didn't matter, you little fool. I took his blood and ended his life."

"How did you even know what he was?"

"When I tortured the poor boy, it didn't take much for his mother's uglier side to come out. I admit, I was pretty freaked out when she bared her fangs. It was only a matter of time before I discovered how I could get my own slice of vampire pie. Rosalee begged me not to take her son's life. I damn near bled him dry. At that point, she was willing to tell me anything." Raúl shrugged. "Even though she spilled every last detail, I still took Ion's life. The bitch needed to be taught a lesson. As for Kane, I'm not finished with him by a long shot. The son of a bitch took my brother's life."

"You took his son, you crazy fuck," Draven chimed in. "I'd call that even."

"I'm no more done with him than he is with me. Rumor has it, he's still gunning for me. What a surprise he'll get when he shows up and I've turned every last one of my men into my own vampire army." Raúl grabbed the decanter of whisky from the table and poured himself a tumbler. "I'd offer you some, but you won't live long enough to enjoy it."

Brea's gaze heated. "You would kill me?"

Raúl ran a hand down his jaw. "I was referring to your friend, *chiquita*. You, I plan to keep."

"I'm not a possession, Raúl. You can't just decide to keep me. I won't stay. Draven is my mate—"

Raúl hissed. "You don't fucking learn, *chiquita*. Now you give me no choice but to kill him. No one stands in my way of getting what I want. I thought I made myself clear last time."

As if to prove his point, he flipped the heavy dining room table. It crashed upside down on the floor, sending glass shards tinkling against the tile. The aroma of good whisky clung to the air.

Raúl's black gaze landed on the two men by the door. "Kill him. The girl comes with me."

"Like hell." In the blink of an eye, Draven leaped onto one of the men by the door, his large fangs sinking into his throat. The man's scream rent the air as the other trained his gun on the back of Draven's skull.

"Kill him, damn it." He grabbed Brea by the hair and pulled her toward the staircase.

Brea lashed out, raking her nails down one of Raúl's cheeks. Blood ran trailed down his dark flesh before the wound quickly began to heal.

Her godfather struck her across the face, snapping her head back.

"Bastard!" she cried.

A gunshot went off behind her, stopping her from further lashing out, and damn near halting her heart. She whipped around. Instead of seeing Draven dead on top of the man he had ripped the throat from, he carried the second one by the throat, slamming his skull against the wall. Plaster cracked and fell to the floor from the impact, loosening the man's hand on the Ruger. It clattered to the floor. Blood ran down Draven's shoulder blade where the bullet had struck. Thankfully, it hadn't been a kill shot.

Raúl wrapped his beefy forearm about Brea's neck, nearly cutting off her oxygen, and hauled her against his massive chest. She was no match for his strength. "Let him go, *pendejo*."

Draven glanced their way, his fingers still wrapped tight around the tall man's throat. Blood coated Draven's mouth and cheeks, dripping from his chin. Brea's gut clenched at the vision before her and what she had turned the barkeep into. He had been nothing but kind in his quest to help, and now he looked like a blood-crazed madman.

"You kill him and she dies."

CHAPTER TWENTY

A RED HAZE COLORED HIS VISION. FURY SLOWLY BURNED UP his spine, holding him taut in its grip like the talons of an eagle. Raúl wrapped his thick forearm around Brea's throat, threatening to take her very life. Her godfather could easily squeeze the breath from her, causing her to pass out. But the lack of oxygen wouldn't kill her. No, he'd have to separate her head from her body. Draven wasn't about to test the man's considerable strength. He had a few more years of vampirism under his belt than Brea.

Draven needed to weigh his options, assess the situation. Anger would cause him to act in haste, make mistakes. He couldn't afford a lapse in judgment. He needed to think clearly, formulate a plan. If he dropped his hold on the tall man's neck, the man would be able to use the assault rifle strapped to his back, put a bullet clean through his heart and finish what the other man failed to do. At this close of range, there wasn't much of a chance that he'd miss.

The second option would be to break the fucker's neck and drop him like a rag doll to the terracotta tiles. Draven much preferred the second option, but he couldn't chance Raúl's counteraction. He'd never forgive himself should the kingpin take his mate's life because he had failed to follow direction. Hell, his life wouldn't be worth living. If Raúl took

127

Brea's life, Draven would go out like *Butch Cassidy and the Sundance Kid*. And he'd take as many of these fuckers with him as he could.

Starting with the piece of shit in his grasp.

"Draven, my man. You look as if you got your hands full at the moment." Draven's gaze followed the sound of the familiar voice. What the hell? Spike strode into the dining room, stopping just shy of the dead man lying at his feet. When Draven turned this black gaze on the Devil, Spike's gaze widened. "What the fuck?"

Raúl hissed, tightening his hold on Brea. Her fingernails dug into her godfather's arm as she struggled against his hold. "I ordered you upstairs. You have an issue with following orders, *chico*? Where's Cisco?"

"Right behind you, boss. I figured you could use the help." Francisco trained his AK47 on the center of Draven's chest. "Release Louis."

Draven dropped his hold, not seeing much choice in the matter and maybe buying them a little more time to come up with a *Plan C*. Louis grabbed his neck, wheezing as he gulped in much-needed air. The odds in their favor had just gone down considerably.

Spike stood in the center of the chaos, looking from Raúl to Brea, stopping back on Draven. "What the hell is in the water? We got some serious ass shit going on. Vampires? Well, I'll be damned."

Spike actually laughed, not freaking out at the paranormal scene he had just happened upon. No, he looked about, a sadistic smile making his grisly self even uglier. He turned back to Raúl. "I don't know how you managed this blood-sucker shit, but I want in."

"You don't even know what the fuck you're asking for, Spike." Louis nudged Draven with the barrel of the gun toward the center of the room within reach of Spike.

Draven growled but kept his hands to himself … for now. "I hate to tell you this, asshole, but now that you know what Raúl is, no way he's letting you walk out of here alive. You should have stayed upstairs."

The biker looked at Raúl. "That true?"

"Depends."

"On?" Spike continued to prod. The idiot just couldn't help himself.

"Your ability to keep your mouth shut."

"You letting me drink from the water?" Spike rubbed his hands together. "If so, I'll keep my mouth shut. This could be some serious ass fun."

If Draven could distract Raúl, he believed he could take out Spike, Louis, and Francisco with little effort. *Plan C* began to form. He looked to Brea, who stilled in Raúl's hold. Draven prayed she played along.

"Why not take her upstairs, Raúl? You got me. No way I'm walking out of here alive." The gun at his back nudged him forward again. He stumbled as if proving his point. "There's no need for her to see this go down."

"Draven—" Raúl's arm tightened.

"Do yourself a favor and get her the fuck out of here, Raúl. She watches me die, and you'll earn her hate."

"Yeah, Raúl," Spike taunted, snarling. "Take her pretty little ass out of here. I got dibs for seconds."

Her godfather's complexion darkened. He bared his long razor-sharp fangs. "I should take your head where you stand, *chico*. Brea belongs to me. No one touches her but me. *¿Comprende?*"

Spike held his hands up. "Relax. It was just a joke. Take her upstairs. What's about to go down isn't for her eyes. I'm going to help take out the garbage. When I'm done, we'll talk about you getting me a pair of those kick ass fangs."

Raúl must have finally seen the wisdom in shielding Brea from watching Draven take his last breath. Backing her from the room, Brea started fighting and kicking like a hellcat, making Draven proud. But in the end, her godfather's strength far outmatched hers. Raúl's hold wasn't giving.

Once they rounded the corner and were out of sight, Draven turned, taking in the three remaining players. Spike didn't have a gun, making him the least of the threats. Louis and Francisco, on the other hand, each had an assault rival aimed at his chest. Draven heard Brea call out to him, just before he heard the sound of flesh hitting flesh and a door slamming closed. Fuck! When he was done with these three, he was going to enjoy killing Raúl … very fucking slowly. The man didn't deserve a swift death.

Time to pay the piper.

Draven turned and stepped toward the biker. "You ever get the feeling of foreboding, Spike?"

The dirtbag chuckled. "I'm betting you're sorry you ever got tangled up with the cartel, huh? I have yet to *thank you* properly for turning the Devils into the DEA yet, asswipe. You and Rogue, you're both going down."

"Not. Going. To. Happen."

The smile never left Spike's face. As a matter of fact, he had no way of seeing what was coming. Draven moved with lightning speed, pulling Spike in front of him, holding him like a shield. Both rifles fired in his direction. The biker's body jerked as the first round of bullets riveted him. Draven tossed him like a sack of dirt at the smaller of the two men, then tackled Louis, ripping out his throat before he had a chance to utter a sound.

A bullet caught Draven in the back, tearing through his lung and causing him to hiss. Moving with precision, he grabbed the other man by the head and twisted hard, easily snapping his neck. Draven's breath sawed out of him as his lung already began to heal. He glanced around at the carnage. Raúl's men were both dead, and Spike was not far from it. Draven could've finished him off, but he preferred the fucker die slowly, to bleed out.

Spike didn't deserve his mercy.

Skirting the bodies and the upended table, he headed for the stairs, taking them two at a time. He didn't want to alert Raúl by calling out, though they'd likely hear his footsteps on the stairs. At the top landing, he paused, listening for a sound, anything to indicate which room he had taken Brea. Silence greeted him. Jogging down the long hall, Draven opted for the door at the end—what he hoped to be the master suite.

He opened the door with such force, the knob slammed against the interior wall and stuck into the plaster. The bedroom was dark, his enhanced sight told him it was also empty. The sound of running water drew his gaze to the entrance of the en suite. Light spilled beneath the closed door. Ripping it from the hinges, he found Brea pale and fully submerged, unmoving beneath the surface of the Jacuzzi's water.

"Jesus!"

Draven slid across the floor and dropped to his knees, pulling Brea from the oversized tub. He laid her upon the white marble tile and began pumping her sternum until water spewed from her lungs. Brea coughed and gulped for air.

"You okay?"

She quickly nodded, holding her throat.

"Where is he?" Draven asked, turning the knobs and shutting off the flow of the water.

Brea coughed again, attempting to clear her water-logged throat. Finally, she said, "I don't know. He … he strangled me until I passed out. I couldn't stop him. He's strong, Draven. He has Kane's blood lineage."

"I'll stop him, Brea. Mark my words. I'll take him out the way same way he took out Kinky … right between the fucker's eyes."

Draven jumped to his feet and sprinted back down the hall, leaping from the landing to the floor below, and into to the dining area, hoping to get to the assault rifles left behind before Raúl got his hands on them. He skidded to a halt. Three men lay dead on the terracotta tiles, their blood already congealing. Raúl's men. The back door was wide open, swinging in the slight breeze, with no sign of Raúl or the fatally wounded Spike.

"Son of a bitch."

CHAPTER TWENTY-ONE

"WHAT FUCK?" KALEB JAMMED A HAND THROUGH HIS short curly hair. "When the hell did I lose control?"

Kane chuckled. "Calm down, bro. It's not as bad as it seems."

"Really?" He looked at Draven and Brea, his hand indicating the guilty party. "We have two vampires that shouldn't exist—"

"Three … actually." Draven couldn't help reminding him of Raúl's vampire status.

Draven liked Kaleb, he did, but at times such as this he seemed a wee bit over the top in dramatics. Okay, so technically, Kaleb should've heard about Brea long before this. As for him, he should have gotten permission to be turned and maybe even thought about joining up with the Sons of Sangue. But hell, that wasn't his life. And truthfully, he was quite happy running the bar and managing the donor society. He didn't need to be a member of the MC to do that.

As for Raúl…

"Don't fucking remind me! Vlad gets word of this and we'll all be toast." Kaleb perched his fists onto his hips. "One of the worst pieces of shit on this planet, and he's a fucking vampire. This ain't going to be good on any level. More like a colossal disaster."

Kane stood, ignoring his twin's theatrics, and skirted the large table in the meeting room of the clubhouse. He held out his hand to Draven, which he took, giving him a half hug and slap on the back of the shoulder. "Welcome, bro. Ignore Hawk. He's having a meltdown."

Kane chuckled, winked at Brea, then pulled her into his embrace. "Cara's going to love you. We'll get you all intro-duced after we're done in here. I'm sure we have some ears to the door out there wondering what's going on. Too bad they can't hear a damn thing through that wood."

"We should call, Vlad." Kaleb regained Kane's attention.

"We should and we will, Hawk." Kane walked over to him and draped his arm over his shoulders. "How about we let the dust settle first. You need to calm the fuck down and we need to welcome these two into the fold."

"We never talked about patching him over," Kaleb said, which he didn't seem all that happy about.

Draven was perfectly fine with not wearing rockers.

"About that, Hawk." He stepped forward. "With all due re-spect, I'd rather not. Not that I don't respect the hell out of you guys, but I'm happy running my bar, providing donors. I'd rather leave all the MC excitement to you guys. If that's okay, I've had enough excitement for a good long while."

Kaleb sighed, looking relieved of not having to call a meet-ing and put to a vote what to do with him. "I'm sure you have."

Draven wrapped one arm behind Brea's back and tucked her against his side. "Brea's had enough as well. If it's all right with the rest of you, we're here if you need us. We got your back, man—but Brea and I need some time to get to know one another. Hell, she still needs to come to terms with Kinky's death and put him to rest. Not to mention she has to get used to the fact she's mated to my sorry ass."

Brea looked up at him and smiled. Draven's heart melted right there, a big old puddle of goo. When the hell had he lost his balls? She placed a hand over his heart. "You big dumb fool, I fell in love with you back at the cabin."

Draven smiled. Big as could be. He couldn't man up and hide that shit if he wanted to. He pulled Brea into his embrace and slanted his lips over hers, kissing her deeply, earning him an instant hard-on and a set of big ass fangs for his actions.

"Whoa," Kaleb spoke up. "You two need to get a fucking room. Seriously. I don't need to see that shit."

Draven stepped back and looked into Brea's warm eyes. He couldn't miss the truth he saw there. She loved his big dumb ass. "Man, I fucking love this woman. I've been enamored with you from the moment you stepped into my bar. Falling in love with you was the easiest thing I've ever done."

"And the smartest." She chuckled. "Can we go home?"

"As in my apartment?"

"That is if you don't mind me moving in."

Draven crushed her to him and kissed her again, one filled with possession. *His.* God, how he loved the sound of that.

He never thought he'd see the day when just one woman would own his heart.

"Let's go get your stuff."

Kane cleared his throat. "There is one more matter we do need to deal with. *Raúl*. You know he's going to come gunning for you two. He's far from done. Does he or anyone else know where you live?"

"Just my bartender, who manages the Blood 'n' Rave. Other than that, no." He shook his head. "I always kept my life private from the bar. I've never even taken a woman there before Brea."

"We need to keep that on the down-low to keep you two safe. If word gets out and Raúl learns your whereabouts, we'll move you into the clubhouse. Xander and Wolf can bunk."

"Like hell," Alexander Dumitru said, striding into the room in time to hear who he might be rooming with if things got hairy and Raúl came to town. Grigore "Wolf" Lupie and Ryder Kelley were quick on his heels. The three men bunked at the clubhouse, having just gotten the bachelor pad back after Kaleb and Grayson "Gypsy" Gabor moved their women and families out.

Kaleb growled. "Can you not follow directions? This is a private church meeting."

"Which involves all of us if the La Paz cartel kingpin is involved." Alexander crossed his thick arms over his chest. "Looks like Pleasant is about to get a whole lot more interesting."

"If Raúl finds out Draven and Brea are back in town and where they are hanging their head," Kaleb said, "we'll need to protect them against him and his men, not to mention Spike and the Devils."

"We're here for our friends. No doubt about that. But Ryder and Wolf can bunk up if need be. No one's bunking in my room. India has dibs on my bed for the time being. I'm on the couch."

"When the fuck did that happen?" Kaleb all but growled. "Why the hell am I just now hearing about this?"

Alexander hid a smile, the twinkle in his eyes giving him away. "It was *a need to know* basis. And since I have yet to figure out what the hell is going on, other than offering her my friendship through her pregnancy—"

"What the fuck? Yours?"

Kaleb looked ready to kill someone. Draven thought maybe Alexander would be better off backing up. Instead, the biker held his ground.

"You really aren't thinking clearly, P." Alexander laughed, not at all offended by Kaleb's ugly mood. "She's not a vamp. I can't get her pregnant. Besides, I'm not sleeping with her."

"Keep it that fucking way." Kaleb glared. "Who's the baby daddy?"

"I have no idea. She's not talking."

Rubbing his jaw, he said. "We will talk about this later. At a proper church meeting."

Alexander nodded, wisely saying nothing further. Draven figured Kaleb had been pushed far enough for one day.

Learning about Raúl's vampire status was more than enough, add in Draven and Brea into the mix, was certainly cause for a spike in his blood pressure.

Time to leave the Sons to their business.

Draven had other *business* he was more than ready to attend to, having to do with the little lady tucked at his side and a set of pristine white sheets. Thank goodness the filthy little cabin was left behind. He was ready to make love to Brea properly. Just the thought had his dick straining the front of his jeans.

"You guys look like you have a lot to talk about." Draven looked down at Brea. "I think it's past time I take my mate home."

Kane walked over and placed a hand on Brea's shoulder. "Go, get some rest. We'll introduce you to our mates later. No need to listen to Hawk's tirades."

Draven shook Kane's hand, said his good-byes, then led Brea from the clubhouse. He opened the passenger door to his Chevy Camaro, glad to have his car back. Thankfully, it had still been parked right where they had left it before trekking through the woods in Mexico. Brea slid inside, looking very much at home there. He was definitely going to like having her around.

He walked around the vehicle and got in behind the wheel, starting the car. The engine rumbled to life. He placed his hands on the gear shift between the seats. Brea reached over and covered his hand with her tinier one.

"You ready for this?" she asked him.

Draven looked into her beautiful face, thinking he'd never been more ready. He had finally found the one woman he'd love waking up to. Every day.

"What's that, sweetheart?"

"You. Me. Us." She squeezed his hand. "And this crazy thing we call life."

Draven reversed the car, then shifted into gear, and headed out of the parking lot, sending gravel flying in his wake. "Sweetheart, I didn't know it, but I've been waiting for us my entire fucking life. Now how about we get home and see what we can do about dirtying up my sheets?"

"Spoken like a true man in love."

He turned to her briefly and winked. "Give me about fifteen minutes to get you and this car home, and I'll show you just how much. Besides, I think I still owe you a steak dinner."

"I'll pass on the steak and settle on the how much." Brea laughed. She moved her hand to his thigh and ran it up his leg, cupping his erection. "Peddle to the floor, babe."

And he did, sending the Camaro flying down the highway, heading for Florence. His home … their home. Damn, if he didn't really love the sound of that.

ABOUT THE AUTHOR

A daydreamer at heart, Patricia A. Rasey, resides in her native town in Northwest Ohio with her husband, Mark, and her two lovable Cavalier King Charles Spaniels, Todd and Buckeye. A graduate of Long Ridge Writer's School, Patricia has seen publication of some her short stories in magazines as well as several of her novels.

When not behind her computer, you can find Patricia working, reading, watching movies or MMA. She also enjoys spending her free time at the river camping and boating with her husband and two sons. Ms. Rasey is currently a third degree Black Belt in American Freestyle Karate.

19281603R00090

Printed in Great Britain
by Amazon